BROWNING P.I.

*Also by Peter Corris
and available in Blacklist*

The Azanian Action

blacklist.

BROWNING P.I.

PETER CORRIS

Angus&Robertson
An imprint of HarperCollins*Publishers*

AN ANGUS & ROBERTSON BOOK
An imprint of HarperCollinsPublishers

First published in Australia in 1992 by
CollinsAngus&Robertson Publishers Pty Limited (ACN 009 913 517)
A division of HarperCollinsPublishers (Australia) Pty Limited
25-31 Ryde Road, Pymble NSW 2073, Australia

HarperCollinsPublishers (New Zealand) Limited
31 View Road, Glenfield, Auckland 10, New Zealand

HarperCollinsPublishers Limited
77-85 Fulham Palace Road, London W6 8JB, United Kingdom

Copyright © Peter Corris 1992

This book is copyright.
Apart from any fair dealing for the purposes of private study,
research, criticism or review, as permitted under the Copyright
Act, no part may be reproduced by any process without written
permission. Inquiries should be addressed to the publishers.

National Library of Australia
Cataloguing-in-Publication data.

Corris, Peter, 1942–
Browning P.I.
ISBN 0 207 17415 6
I. Title
A823.3

Cover: Jet *(1989)* by Robyn Stacey
cibachrome, 1.05 x 1.85m
Courtesy of Robyn Stacey and the Mori Gallery
Typeset in Australia by Midland Typesetters
Printed in Australia by The Book Printer
5 4 3 2 1
95 94 93 92

For Stuart Coupe

1

Not many men have had the misfortune to count among their enemies the FBI *and* Errol Flynn. I did and it caused me a lot of trouble in the early 1940s. The FBI reneged on the deal we'd struck after I helped them expose the Ku Klux Klanners in Hollywood and, like other foreigners, I had to go to Canada to clear myself with the immigration people. I could register there as an Australian, apply for entry to the US where I had a guarantee of employment (I was working on *Gentleman Jim* for Warners with Raoul Walsh directing and Flynn playing James J. Corbett), and sail along in the Californian sun for another few years.

'How old are you, Dick?' Flynn said as we were having a drink during a break in the filming.

'Err, thirty-four, Errol,' I said. Which was putting it back a bit, but I always looked younger than my age when I was in shape. At that time I was because I'd been boxing in the gym for the previous few months, mostly taking punishment from Flynn and others. 'Why?'

'Nothing. Think I might come up to Canada with you. Be good to hear the King's English spoken again.'

I don't know where he got that idea. Canadians talked pretty much like Americans to my ear, the ones who didn't talk like Frenchmen, but Flynn never was the brightest. Anyway, we got to Toronto and I filled in the forms and waited outside the offices and did all the other things you have to do to get bureaucrats to earn their pay. The day it was all wrapped up I got drunk with Flynn in a bar on Queen Street West.

'Canada's in the war, y'know,' Flynn said. 'Like Australia. Do you miss it, Dick?'

'What?' I said.

Flynn tossed back his drink and signalled for another. He drank as if every drop might be his last. 'Australia,' he said, when he had a full one in front of him. 'The wide brown land. How's it go again? "I love the sunburnt country, the land of endless plains[1]..."'

'Sunburnt is right,' I said. 'Did you ever spend any time in the bush? Bloody godforsaken... No fear, I don't miss it. California'll do me.'

'Still,' Flynn mused, 'the empire's under threat. We should be doing our bit.'

It was on the tip of my tongue to tell him I'd done my bit in the piece of lunacy they called the Great War, but that would've given away my age. I drank and said nothing. We went on drinking and Flynn kept nagging away about Australia and patriotism and the British race. I tried to tell him I was mostly Irish, like himself, but somehow he got under my skin. That was one of his talents, egging people on into doing things they normally wouldn't have dreamed of doing. Of course the alcohol helped. The upshot was that we both staggered into a recruiting depot and presented ourselves as members of the jolly old British Empire, ready to die for King and country.

Flynn was about thirty at this time and the booze hadn't yet turned him into a rotting hulk. The medical wouldn't be a problem for him. Nor, as it turned out, for me. Although I was over forty and had lived a hard life I had the constitution of a man fifteen years younger. My papers were in order; I passed the medical with flying colours (the doctors must have been instructed to ignore alcohol levels) and was inducted into the Canadian army.

It's not quite as mad as it sounds. The war hadn't got fully under way, Canada wasn't sending men overseas[2], and I was pretty sure I'd be able to complete the picture before I had to get into khaki. Besides, I was confused. I suppose I had visions of strutting about— Captains Flynn and Browning, an entertainment unit maybe, giving speeches, raising money, screwing women in and out of uniform. Flynn would be pulling every string in sight, I was sure of that.

I came down with a thump when I saw Flynn leaning against a wall in the recruitment office, hands in pockets, smoking and talking to a Canadian major. A sergeant marched up behind me, crashed his boots down and ordered me to stand to attention. I did it and all my old fear and hatred of the army came back to me in a rush. Very sobering.

'Errol, old boy,' I stammered, 'well, we've done it, eh?'

Then I realised that Flynn wasn't nearly as drunk as he'd made out. He looked at me with those hard, grey eyes. '*You've* done it, Dick. Afraid I struck a snag.'

'What d'you mean?'

'Quite forgot that I became an American citizen a while back. Slipped my mind. It's the US army for me, worse luck. God knows when we'll get into the stoush.'

The sergeant marched me away and they had to practically lift me into the truck that took us to boot camp. Errol Flynn. Jesus, how I hated that man. I spent almost two years in the Canadian army, mostly in the tank corps. I still can't look at a tank without feeling sick—horrible machines, tanks, either freezing cold or sizzling hot. I was an acting sergeant for a time which was bearable, but after I got busted for drunkenness when on duty it was endless parades and days of peeling potatoes. Eventually I convinced a halfway human doctor that I was unfit for service and I was invalided out. No pension though.

I went back to Hollywood and it was working on *Murder, My Sweet* with Dick Powell and Claire Trevor that gave me the idea of setting up as a private detective. Mind you, I'd met a few men who practised the trade around LA. They were nothing like the guys on the screen. They were ex-cops, ex- and not so ex-drunks, seedy types to a man. I don't mean the big agency boys— the Pinkertons and such. They were professionals and pretty dull. I mean the shamuses.

I'd seen a lot of private eye movies, enough, anyway, to know that they were malarkey. You only had to take a look at Hammett and Chandler themselves to know that they weren't tough guys and wouldn't know what tough was. Bogart and Alan Ladd were tough in their way but neither of them was over five-foot-six. It was all make-believe. My idea was this: try to bring the make-believe and the reality closer together. I had in mind the blondes and the drinks and the rich clients, not the gunplay. How hard could it be? I thought.

Follow wandering husbands and wives, snap a few pictures, drape the six-foot-two-inch frame in a well-cut suit and cultivate a hard look.

I had my discharge papers from the Canadian army which were like a personal reference from the King of England just then. I looked like a soldier, always had, and I carried enough scars to make the role convincing. I could walk with a half-genuine limp when I remembered. Character references from Jack Warner himself, N. Robert Silkstein my agent, who was a great war bonds salesman, my army papers and the payment of my liability fee were enough to get me a ticket to operate as a private enquiry agent in the state of California. To get a gun licence I had to convince the cops I could shoot. I convinced them.

I figured that Los Angeles, with half the able-bodied men away and the other half scared of going, with most of the women working and everyone with more money than they ever had before in their lives, would be a honey pot. I should have stayed at Warners as a bit player or got on the first boat out of San Pedro for Argentina...

I've never read any of Raymond Chandler's novels, but people who have tell me they're pretty good. Plenty of jokes, they say, good plots, descriptions of LA the way it was in the forties and lots of good-looking women. That sounds all right and maybe I'll get around to reading some of them one of these days. God knows there aren't many of those things around in the movies any more, and still less on TV. So maybe I'll break the habit of a lifetime and settle down some night with a book instead of a bottle.

Chandler himself liked a joke as I recall, and could even take one against himself, which is rare. It had to be the right kind of crack though, preferably with Latin in it. Jokes about how short he was or the age of his wife or any kind of story with a homosexual in it didn't go down well with him at all. I remember one time when Pete McVey said to him, 'Ray, what do you get when you cross a faggot with an ostrich?'

You think that kind of joke is new? You're wrong. They were telling them in Hollywood in 1944. I can't remember what Chandler said. Maybe he didn't say anything. He probably just puffed on his pipe and looked wise. He was good at that. I can't remember the punchline either, so it can't have been very good. Maybe it'll come to me as I get on with the story. We had Raymond Chandler as a client for a while. When I say 'we' I mean me and Pete who ran this detective agency in LA for a short time. We were partners... I'd better start at the beginning.

I'd opened a small-time detective agency in May 1944, working out of my apartment in the Wilcox Hotel on the corner of Wilcox Avenue and Selma, a block from Hollywood Boulevard. I had one room with a Murphy bed and a small desk. With the bed folded up there was just enough room for me to position the desk so that I could sit on one side with the client on the other. I also had a kitchenette so I didn't have to make coffee on the desk or keep the bottles inside the bed. I was in the book and ran a cheap ad in a couple of papers from time to time, but the set-up was from hunger which anyone could see. Consequently, I didn't get many clients.

But I hadn't given up on the movie business either. I got a small part once in a while. I was in a barroom scene in *The Lost Weekend* and I had a line in *Dillinger*, before I got hit with a hail of machine-gun bullets. It was hard to combine the two jobs and I missed a few clients on account of being in a movie and lost out on some movie work because I was driving around looking for a lost wife or a writer of rubber cheques. When I say that the rent at the Wilcox was only ninety bucks a month and I sometimes had trouble making it, you'll get some idea of the state of business.

To tell the truth, I was a lousy detective. I was bad in a number of ways but you could sum it up by saying I gave up too easily. Flaw in my character, that. I can still hear the sports master at Dudleigh bellowing, 'Go in, Browning. You have to want the ball!' Well, I didn't want it, not if it meant getting my fingers broken and my brains beaten out. Same thing with detecting. I'd drive around those hot LA streets, tracking people down from one deadbeat address to another. Sometimes I got lucky and found the guy or the woman and they were happy to be found. I'd get paid and feel good. But more often the trail would go cold or, worse, get closer and closer to East LA where the blacks and Mexicans lived and a white detective in a suit and driving a 1940 Olds was about as welcome as a blowfly on a pavlova[3].

I was sitting with my feet on the desk and a Camel in my mouth reading about Lupe Velez in the *Examiner* when Pete McVey knocked and came straight in. Did I say there was room for me and a client in the room? That was only true if the client was on the small side. Pete wasn't. He must've stood two or three inches taller than me and weighed another fifty pounds. That made a lot of beef in one small room. I took my feet off the desk. My first thought was that he'd come to take money off me or do me harm. Much the same thing. He wore a crumpled brown suit and a hat with a wide brim. When he took the hat off I could see black spiky hair and a face that looked as if his mother and father were very ill-matched. He had a soft, baby-faced look about him until you saw that his eyes were iron grey and as hard as rivets.

He dropped the hat on the desk, giving me so much less room for my feet. He sat down, which he managed by tucking his knees up under his chin. 'Too bad about Lupe,' he said.

Conversation was better than assault and battery. I felt I had to keep my end up. 'Did you know her?'

'Not as well as some guys. You?'

I grinned. 'Better than some guys, not as well as others.'

That drew a smile. The smile was softer than the eyes, just. He stuck his hand out and his arm easily stretched across the desk. He had about a half yard of forearm; you'd need a telephone book to build yourself up to Indian wrestle with him. His grip was nothing Johnny Weismuller wouldn't have been able to handle.

8

'Pete McVey,' he said. 'In the same racket as you but doing a little better.'

'That wouldn't be hard,' I said. It was an Australian sort of remark, reflecting more on me than him, but Americans never seem to know how to take that and he scowled as he took a cigarette from my pack on the desk.

I slid my lighter across to him as a peace offering and he lit up and looked at me through the smoke. 'I'm doing a little job for Robert Silkstein. Believe you know him?'

I was hurt. He was my agent. What was he doing hiring some other private detective? 'I know him,' I said.

McVey fanned smoke away politely. 'Yeah. Well, Silkstein's got this writer client, Hart Sallust. Hell of a name.'

'He's a hell of a writer,' I said, 'and a hell of a drinker.'

McVey stubbed out his butt in the old Senior Service cigarette tin I used for an ashtray. 'That's where you come in. Sallust is missing and he's coming up very close to the deadline to deliver a script.'

I stubbed out my cigarette too; the only difference was I lit another one straight off. 'He'll make it. He always does. He drinks like his throat might be going to close up on him any minute, but he gets the writing done. Christ knows how. I've spent a fair bit of time with him and I've never actually seen him do any typing, but the scripts hit the desks.'

'I like the "actually",' McVey said. 'You British?'

'Australian. They talk English there some of the time. What's got Bobby so riled up?'

'It appears he hasn't seen diddly squat of this script. Usually Sallust shows him how it's coming along. This time, nothing.'

I shrugged. 'Sallust is one of the best. The studio'll wait.'

'Uh-uh, it's a thing for Garfield, and he's going into the army in a couple of months.'

'He's Silkstein's client too,' I said. 'Bobby's looking at a major loss here.'

'That's right. Now Silkstein allows you know Sallust, know where he boozes, the kinds of broads he favours, where he's likely to flop.'

'Mmm.'

McVey looked around the room, taking in the thin carpet, the foldup bed and the closet with the silver flaking off the mirror on its door. I could tell he wasn't impressed by the tin ashtray either. 'If I had something to drink on me, would you have something for us to drink out of?'

It was getting on for noon and the talk about drinking had made me thirsty. Hart Sallust's name had added to the effect. When you thought of Sallust you just naturally thought of beer and whiskey and wine and about any damn thing with alcohol in it. I moved pretty fast out to the kitchenette and came back with two fairly clean glasses. McVey took a flat pint out of the pocket of his suit jacket, ripped off the seal and poured.

He said, 'Here's mud in your eye,' and sipped.

I said, 'Cheers,' and took a solid drink. It was rye, not good rye, but good enough. I took another solid drink which left my glass empty, the way they will get.

McVey passed the bottle across the desk. I poured another shot. 'Your whiskey's okay,' I said. 'But maybe I should see some identification and your ticket before I do any more talking.'

He nodded with what looked like approval and fished out his wallet. He showed me his licence, carrying a serial number a good deal lower than mine, indicating that he'd been in the business longer. I handed it back and he put it away. You'd feel that wallet on your hip; there was a comfortable-looking amount of money in it. I felt encouraged and wondered if I should try another sentence using actually.

McVey took another small sip of his drink. 'Silkstein said you weren't going to set the world on fire as a detective but that you were reasonably honest.'

'Big of him,' I said, which was funny if you knew Bobby. He was barely five-foot-four in his lifts. McVey got the joke and smiled. We were getting along fine. Well enough to have another drink maybe.

'He also said that he'd be damned if he was going to put you on expenses to go looking for Sallust. He said it'd be like ... I can't remember his expression, but he meant something like putting a hog in a cornfield.'

I was offended of course, but I was still thinking of that money and couldn't afford to show it. 'I gather you're a country boy, McVey.'

'Idaho.'

'You're a long way from home, like me.'

'Glad of it, too. You ever been to Idaho?'

'I don't think so. I've travelled a lot, but I don't think so.'

'No reason to remember it. Nothing happens there worth noticing. I prefer it here, even if half the people you meet are slime.'

That wasn't quite so hopeful a note, but I had the drink anyway. 'So how can I help you, as one professional to another?'

'We can team up to find Sallust. You know the places to look. I'll keep you off the sauce and we'll split the fee. What do you say?'

2

My yellow Olds was parked on Wilcox and I went towards it automatically. McVey shook his head and steered me in the direction of a grey Packard parked near the post office.

'Why don't you have a two-tone convertible with a whip aerial and a coon tail?' he said.

I explained that I'd bought the car a few years back with some movie earnings and that it was appropriate at the time.

He grunted. 'A man in this line of work needs a quiet-looking car. Unobtrusive. Driving that you couldn't follow a blind man in a wheelchair.'

I could have said that around Beverly Hills and some other places, where they go in for personalised paint jobs on their cars, his Packard would have looked out of place. I could have said that. But for one thing I didn't do much work in those places and for another I like to be easy to get on with. Especially when a man's bought me three pretty good drinks and has some money in his pocket that's almost mine. I didn't say anything, just settled into the passenger seat and let McVey squeeze himself in behind the wheel. He pressed the starter and the engine caught as if it wanted to make the car airborne.

'Tune her myself,' McVey said. 'Don't smoke in the car if you don't mind. Stinks up the interior. Where to?'

I let the cigarette stick there in my mouth unlit while I considered. (Maybe it was at that moment I fell into the habit of playing with cigarettes more than smoking them. I've gone through a pack and a half a day for forty years but I doubt if I've smoked half of them.) It was a hot August afternoon. If Sallust was out on the toot, where would he be? It depended on his mood, which was a very changeable thing. Sometimes he liked to drink in the bars of Greek restaurants, sometimes it was Chinese. He also liked fake Irish pubs, Mexican cantinas and Polish places. He even went into some of the less dangerous coloured joints. When I say less dangerous I don't mean I'd go into them myself, except maybe with someone McVey's size to back me up. It was a comforting thought, until it occurred to me that Silkstein might have had it first.

All that's not to say Sallust wouldn't drink in an ordinary neighbourhood bar or a cocktail lounge. It was all a matter of mood and the stage of the binge he was on. 'When did Bobby last see Sallust?'

McVey pulled a notepad out of his pocket and flipped over the pages. 'Four days ago. He was supposed to be delivering the script. He didn't and Silkstein roasted him. Sallust used some dirty words and walked out. Silkstein called him, even went round to his place. No dice.'

'Was Hart drunk at the time?'

'Silkstein didn't say so. Matters, does it?'

I nodded. 'If he's only three, four days into a bender he'll still be wearing a tie. We'll start at the Players'.'

McVey may have had cornstalks in his hair and axle grease under his fingernails (he didn't, but you know what I mean), but he knew a bit about Hollywood. He headed west towards Sunset. On the way we talked about Lupe Velez, who'd been found dead by her maid. Louella Parsons' black-bordered piece in the paper had described Lupe as 'never lovelier' as she lay on a satin sheet in a lamé gown with the seconal and brandy bottles beside her.

'I heard different,' McVey said. 'I heard she sicked up all over the bedroom and drowned in the john.'

I'd had a one-nighter with Lupe, the 'Mexican Spitfire', some years before. It was hard not to if you wore trousers and could move around a little. I'd liked her and preferred Louella's version. Still, that was no way for a tough detective to feel. 'Nah,' I said, 'if Lupe was going to drown she'd have the class to do it in a silver ice bucket.'

That got me another grin from McVey and then we were outside the Players' Club. Preston Sturgess[4] had opened the place a few years before and made it a hangout for writers and literary types. The Garden of Allah was just over the street and I guess Dottie Parker[5] and Benchley could carry their drinks across. Drinks were what the club was famous for—strong ones—which was why Hart Sallust liked it.

We parked further down the strip and walked back. I had on my best suit, a grey lightweight, and my cleanest shoes and hat. I thought I'd be able to get into the place, at least long enough to ask about Sallust. McVey wouldn't get in on looks or clothes but he had his height, weight and wallet to back him up. We went through the doors just far enough to get a look at the New York, or maybe Chicago atmosphere —lots of leather and potted plants—before being braced. I forget the name of the traffic director, but business was slow and he appeared to be looking around for a table. McVey shook his head and passed me a five. I pressed it into the guy's hand.

'Could you ask in the bar if Hart Sallust has been in lately?'

He took the money but didn't bother to reply. McVey and I kicked our heels in the tiled lobby. Edward G. Robinson brushed past us in a cloud of cigar smoke. He'd probably gone in to look at the club's art collection. I'd heard it was pretty good, but I couldn't tell a Picasso from a Disney. The man who'd taken the money came back and gave us a word for each dollar.

'He was here on Monday.'

Only two days ago. We were hot on his trail. We went back to the car but I didn't get in.

'What?' McVey said.

'I'm thinking, and to do that I need a cigarette.'

We wandered along until we found a palm tree to take shade under. On Sunset in those days that wasn't hard. We stood in a patch of shade and smoked and looked at the people who hurried along the street. They made me feel hot and reminded me that at least as a private detective I didn't have to hurry anywhere most of the time. I also didn't have to wear a jacket. I peeled mine off and draped it over my shoulder. McVey kept his on, no doubt because the holster he wore might have attracted attention.

He dropped his butt and stood on it. 'Well?'

'The Brown Derby,' I said.

He looked up the street towards Vine but I shook my head. 'Not that one. The place on Wiltshire.'

We drove to the original Derby, which was just a lunch counter before it got famous and started to have children. Sallust wasn't there but he had been two days back. That information also cost five bucks. At the other Brown Derby, on Los Filez Boulevard, we were only a day and a half behind him. McVey was making notes of his expenses in a little ledger book he kept in another of his deep pockets.

'I think I'm getting his drift,' I said. 'He follows a kind of pattern. It's called a pub crawl in England.'

'I'd call it a lush trail. Where next?'

From watching private eye pictures and talking to a few of the breed, I'd decided that these fellows ran themselves too hard, never took a break between taking beatings and taking drinks. That wasn't my style even though it looked to be McVey's. Time to stall. 'Nothing to be done now. He'll be flopping somewhere, could be anyplace. Tonight we should be able to find him with a bit of luck. I'll make out a list of places and look at the map. We can be real efficient about it.'

I thought McVey might go for that. He drove me back to the Wilcox and the grip he put on my arm as I was getting out of the car was supposed to remind me who was the boss and it did. 'So, where do we meet and when, Browning?'

'Call me Richard. I'd say Dick but that's the wrong kind of moniker for this business.'

He gave a snort that was half a laugh and half a snarl. 'I reckon I'd run out of breath saying Richard all the time. How's about Rich?'

It sounds strange nowadays, but we exchanged cards. Mine was plain and cheap. It said 'Richard K. Browning, Private Enquiries', with my address and phone number. His had a red border around it and read: 'Peter McVey Agency, Confidential Enquiries'. After his name and before the location details were the letters 'M.A.P.D.A.' I asked him what they stood for.

'Member of the American Private Detectives' Association.'

'I didn't know there was one.'

'There ain't, so far as I know. Where and when, Rich?'

'The Trocadero, Pete,' I said. 'At nine.'

I did some drinking at the Trocadero once in a while. I used to go there a lot when I was working for Hughes on *Hell's Angels* and lounge around in a leather jacket with dress trousers and shirt and be quite the young flyboy hero. Flirted with Swanson, yarned with Coop— that sort of thing. Those days were pretty much behind me now it seemed and, although I didn't know it then, the Troc was on the way out. It closed a year or so after the time I'm talking about. Anyway, as long as I was shaved, wearing a jacket and wasn't too drunk, I was more or less welcome in the place. I turned up in that condition at around nine and found McVey pacing the sidewalk outside the joint.

'You're late,' he said.

I looked at my watch. 'Ten minutes. We're not meeting Sam Goldwyn. I'm not saying Hart'll be here, you know. This is just the first port of call.'

McVey grunted and snapped his cigarette into the gutter. I learned as we went along that he only smoked when he was nervous. 'Time is money. Let's get on it.'

'Talking of money,' I said. 'That wallet of yours hasn't breathed any air in a while. I figure it's time to give it some oxygen.'

He looked at me suspiciously. 'Meaning?'

I took off my hat and smoothed down my hair. I had on a dark suit, cream shirt and a silk tie—all pretty well pressed. McVey had changed his shirt but he still looked like a rumpled rube. Still, so did Gable at times. 'This isn't the kind of place you walk into and buy everything you want with a fin. You have to sit, drink a little, shoot the breeze. Come at it sideways, know what I mean?'

He was nervous. He removed his hat and straightened the brim. No use trying to pat down that spiky hair; it'd spring straight back up again. 'I don't like it. But I'll let you call it for a while. I'm not used to this kind of place.'

'That'll give us something to talk about. C'mon.' We checked our hats and my smile and a buck got us a reasonable table. I ordered a steak and a whiskey sour and McVey ordered a club sandwich and beer. The place was only half full and I didn't see anyone I knew. McVey's eyes bored into every face until I told him to take it easy.

'He ain't here,' he said.

'It's too early. Anyway, how do you know? You've never met him.'

He pulled a photograph from his pocket and put it on the table. It looked like a touched-up studio publicity shot of about twenty years before and resembled Sallust the way a Siamese kitten resembles an alley cat. This Sallust looked soft and vulnerable, ever-so sensitive, with big brown eyes, thick glossy hair and gleaming white teeth. The Sallust I knew had walnut-sized pouches under his eyes, facial grooves you could put cigarettes in and his hair was almost white. His teeth were stained brown from smoking and the two front ones had got chipped in a fight. Fifteen years in Hollywood and every day of it was written on his face.

'Put it away,' I said, 'or someone'll think we're either talent scouts or faggots. Anyway, it doesn't look anything like him.'

The food and drinks arrived and we got started on them. I asked McVey to tell me about himself and how come he had an office in Santa Monica and was doing a job in Hollywood with a technique that belonged in Detroit. The three beers he drank got him talking and the club sandwich didn't stop him. He told me that he'd operated in Philadelphia for twelve years before some spots on his lungs sent him west. That gave us something in common. I'd been a lunger some years back and occasionally spat in a hankie and took a look. He'd been in Santa Barbara for six years, mostly doing what he called 'industrial work'. I knew what that meant—keeping oil-workers in line, repossessing autos and freelancing for insurance companies on false identities, fraudulent claims and torch jobs. Tough work.

The steak was good and so was the whiskey. I kept an eye on the door and ordered another drink. McVey didn't object. He seemed to like drinking beer and talking about himself so I kept him at it.

'How did you get the job from Bobby? No offence, Pete, but there's plenty of detectives in LA.'

He chewed that over with the last bite of his sandwich. When he'd finished swallowing he took a long pull at his beer and wiped his big, red hand across his face. 'I ain't exactly proud of it. I met this girl in a cat house in Santa Barbara. Kinda stumbled over her. Turned out she was this Robert Silkstein's daughter. A runaway.'

I reflected on that. Bobby was in his early forties at the most. He didn't strike me as the type to have married early so the daughter was probably very young. I nodded understandingly.

'Anyway,' McVey said, 'I brought her home. She wanted to come. Just didn't have a good story to tell her folks. She 'n' me cooked up a good one and her Dad and Mom were happy. Silkstein had this problem on his hands and he gave me the job.'

'Fine,' I said. 'We'll make a good team. I know the town and you're big enough to handle anything that gets too much for one man.'

'How tough can it be? He's a writer. Those guys don't exactly chew bricks from what I've heard. Why should they? They've got a good racket. The tough stuff's all in their heads the way it should be. I'm a great reader. Love a good book. You?'

I shook my head and thought about another drink. The beer had made McVey mellow and he'd probably spring for it, but we might have a big night ahead. I started to fill him in on Hart's habit of throwing insults and fists around in low taverns, then I stopped in mid-sentence and stared through the smoke at the door.

McVey was mellow but that's all. His head swivelled. 'What?' he rasped. 'You see him?'

'No,' I said. 'I see a ghost.'

3

Lupe Velez was walking through the smoke haze towards a table to our right. She was wearing a silver lamé dress and a tiara, strutting on four-inch heels that would've lifted her to about five-foot-five. She had a long cigarette holder in a glittering glove and her face was lit up by mischief and martinis. Scarlet lips parted, snowy teeth flashed and she shouted 'Caramba!' in a high-pitched squeal that sounded more like Annapolis than Acapulco.

The shout brought the table of four men behind us to its feet. They started clapping and exclaiming and saying 'darling' a lot. As the lamé and tiara swept past our table I could see the padded chest and too-glossy wig. McVey got it a second later, before the guy was enveloped by his laughing, twittering chums.

'Jesus,' McVey said. 'This town.'

I signalled for another drink. 'David Niven summed it up for me once. He said, "In Hollywood, bad taste is good fun." I think it was Niven. Might've been Laughton.'

'You know those guys?'

Something in McVey's voice made me pay attention to him rather than wonder where the waitress was with my drink. He was bent towards me as if no sound I uttered was to be missed. I remembered then the quick intake of breath I'd heard in the lobby of the Players' club when Robinson had breezed through. It had been Pete, gasping in awe. The guy was screenstruck as well as a bookworm. Strange ways for a private detective. I decided that it was something to exploit. I lit a cigarette and plucked the drink off the tray before the waiter could set it down. 'Sure,' I said. 'Worked with a lot of 'em—Fairbanks, Cooper, Bogart. Still do, from time to time.'

'Bogart,' Pete breathed. 'Errol Flynn too, I bet. You being an Aussie.'

It stuck in my craw to do it, but I nodded and flashed my version of the famous Flynn smile. 'That's right, mate.'

'Jesus,' Pete said. 'I go to the movies all the time. What would I have seen you in, Rich? I have to say I don't remember the name and I read all the credits.'

That was a bit difficult. I had a few small credits but under other names mostly, because of troubles with the immigration and tax people. Truth was, I couldn't remember who I'd been in what. I rattled off the names of a few pictures—*The Frontiersman, Kid Galahad, Sante Fe Trail.* I told him I had a bit in *Lost Weekend* which hadn't been released yet but everyone was talking about already as an Oscar winner[6].

McVey lapped it up. 'You get to talk with Milland?'

I hadn't but what was the point in spoiling his fun? 'I got to drink with him,' I said. 'In the movie.'

McVey shook his head in admiration and ordered another beer. The evening was turning out pretty good and I was beginning to think that if we didn't find Hart Sallust tonight what the hell? We could look for him again tomorrow. I couldn't have been more wrong. McVey gulped down his beer and the steely look came into his eyes rather than the glassy one I suppose was in mine. 'Right,' he said, 'enough of the fun talk. We've had our eats and drinks, time to learn something. Who you going to ask about our boy? The faggots?'

I pulled my mind back onto the job with an effort. 'No. Sallust isn't that way at all. He's girl-crazy.' I corrected myself quickly in case he got the wrong impression. 'Woman-crazy. Wait here, I'll ask around. And keep your coat done up. The butt of that cannon's sticking out halfway across the table.'

I said that just to keep him in his place. I worked the room for fifteen minutes, getting the brush-off here and the half-welcoming grin there. It was a mixed crowd, a lot of movie people, some cattlemen and their girlfriends for twenty-four hours, and honest citizens who'd saved up for a big night out. Ben Hogan was sitting at a table in the corner surrounded by men with stomachs and women with suntans. I drew a blank with the patrons and moved on to question the help in descending order of importance.

Nothing from the barmen or the waitresses. Nothing from the doorman. It was the negro carhop's lucky night. 'Sure, I know Mr Sallust,' he said. 'And I saw him tonight, sir. 'Bout an hour ago.'

I gave him a dollar. 'That's worth a buck. See if you can make it two.'

'He pulled up in a convertible. Looked like he was going to come in but he changed his mind and they drove away.'

Another dollar. 'What kind of car and who was with him?'

'Red Buick two-seater. Had a woman with him who was doing the driving which was just as well.'

'Was Sallust drunk?'

The negro made a see-sawing motion with his hand. I put another note in it.

'Describe the lady.'

He hesitated. I was about to peel off another buck when I heard McVey's voice at my shoulder. 'Describe her,' he growled.

'Chink,' the negro said. 'Or part-Chink. Green silk dress, high collar and cut up the side the way they do. You know?'

I could smell the beer on McVey's breath when he spoke. There was no threat in his attitude and no money in his hand, but he had the negro's attention. 'Sure. They call it a cheong sam or something.'

'I wouldn't know, boss.'

'What kind of a woman was she?' I asked.

He knew what I meant. In 1944 you couldn't ask a negro a question like that about a white woman. He'd clam up for sure. Even a part-Chinese made it a bit dangerous. He reached out and took another dollar from the few I still held. 'Not exactly a lady,' he said. 'Thank you, gentlemen. I got to get back to work.'

McVey handed me my hat and the cigarettes and lighter I'd left on the table. I'd been hoping to go back inside and think about what to do next over a tall, cool one, but that obviously wasn't on. I brushed imaginary dust off the hat and lit one of the cigarettes.

Pete looked at me with amusement. 'Yeah, I can see you in the movies,' he said. 'You do things like that real nice. Can't be that many places in this town you can take a Chinese whore. Where to, Rich?'

I sighed. Hopes of catching the show at Ciro's went out the window. 'Singapore Sam's,' I said.

Singapore Sam's was a nightspot on Sherman Street in Venice. I mean Venice, Los Angeles County. I'd lived there myself five or six years back, managing a boarding house called the Casablanca. Venice was a fun place although it was going rapidly downhill in 1944. The sea air had peeled the paint off most of the buildings long ago and was starting to rot the wood and break down the stucco. All but a few of the canals had been filled in, but Sam's joint was close enough to one that still existed to give it an 'on the water' flavour as long as the wind was in the right direction. If it wasn't, the place had a 'by the trashcan' flavour. There was certainly no problem about taking a Chinese whore to Sam's. The colour bar didn't operate as strongly in Venice as in other places. A mixed-race couple could shack up there without too much trouble, as long as they behaved themselves. As I climbed into McVey's car I reflected that things weren't turning out too badly. You could have a good enough time at Sam's and, unless things had changed in the past few years, Pete and I and Hart Sallust, if he was there, would be the toughest guys around. White guys, that is.

4

The décor at Sam's was red and gold and if the smoke and fumes had got to it over the years that was just part of the atmosphere. The tables tended to be sticky, likewise the carpet and the glasses. You didn't go to Sam's to stay clean and well pressed. But the place had never attracted the rough element—no stuntmen or truck drivers or boxers. As I say, coloured people were tolerated there, even encouraged. Normally this would have led to problems—fights over the women and over insults real and imagined. But Sam had Big Sung to keep things in order.

All you need to know about Sung is that he was a Manchurian who ducked his head and turned sideways to get through the door. He kept order all right. I was worried about Pete's cannon and asked him to leave it in the car. He was disinclined until I told him what Sung had done with a gun once. He had extracted the bullets and made the owner hold them all in his mouth for a minute or so while Sung bent the barrel out of shape. Then he'd given the guy back his gun.

'Tough?' Pete said.

'You bet. Here, we tread very quietly. We ask to see Sam and we tell him politely what we're doing. Chances are he'll let us sit and wait for Hart. We'll have to have a few drinks.'

'You'll hate that.'

I ignored the crack and we went up the steps and in through heavy, ornately carved wooden doors. The room was fairly full and fairly noisy. As usual, it was a very mixed crowd racially and in every other way. There were men present who owned whole blocks of Venice real estate and guys who barely had the price of a room. I forgot to mention there was gambling out back and girls a floor or two above, but that's because it wasn't something to mention. You knew or you didn't. You didn't talk about it, especially not after you'd taken a close look at Sung. He came towards us now, looming up out of the smoke fog like a truck.

'Mr Browning,' he said. 'Good evening.'

'Hello, Sung,' I said. 'My friend and I are here on business.'

I could hear a growl in McVey's throat. That kind of an introduction probably violated every trade rule he loved, but I knew what I was doing. Sung stood in front of us, assessing any threat of possible disturbance and summing us up down to the last dollar. I went on breaking the rules.

'We're hoping Mr Hart Sallust will turn up. We think he might.'

'Sallust.' Sung put some expression into the word —for him this made it an exclamation of astonishment. His hand shot out faster than Ray Robinson's[7] jab. He took hold of my right shoulder and bent it slightly out of shape. 'I think you better have a talk with Mr Sam.'

'Sure, sure,' I said. 'Easy on the shoulder. I keep it for girls to cry on.'

Sung slackened his grip and showed a set of teeth that looked slightly pointed. The word was he filed them, but that was only said jokingly and when he was a safe mile or so out of earshot. He manoeuvred me between tables like a slalom skier. Pete followed, pissed-off, I could sense, but respectful of Sung's size and competence. Briefly I regretted that I'd made him park the gun, but I've learned that regrets are useless and get in the way of saving your ass at the critical moment.

We went through a padded door, down a short, dimly-lit passage.

'You will wait here, please,' Sung said.

I was glad about the 'please'. Pete looked as if he didn't want to kick his heels in a passageway. I tried to look as if it was exactly what I wanted to do.

'Sure,' I said. 'Take your time.'

I leaned against the wall, lit a cigarette and tried to act casual. Pete chewed on a kitchen match and acted agitated. Sung was back in about five minutes. He gave us another one of his smiles and ushered us out of the passage and into another world. It was a sitting room-cum-office, with a desk, easy chairs, coffee table and well-filled bookshelves. Here the lighting was bright enough to see by and the walls were freshly painted. The pictures hanging on three of them looked expensive. There was a polished wood floor with a big, thick oriental rug and a light smell of incense in the air. Singapore Sam was behind the desk, playing with a paperknife. In one of the chairs, sitting with her legs drawn up, was the most beautiful woman I'd ever seen in my life. Maybe Sung was still holding on to me, I didn't know. Maybe he was still hurting me, I didn't care. I couldn't take my eyes off her.

'Richard, my friend,' Sam drawled. 'So nice to see you and your friend. Sung, why are you treating Mr Browning like a plucked chicken?'

Sung said something in a language I took to be Chinese. The woman's head jerked up and she stared at me. Sam stared, too. A slight tilt of Sam's head and Sung let me go. Another tilt and he went out of the room—two hundred and twenty pounds of bone and muscle moving like an oiled rifle bolt.

'Sit down, gentlemen, and have some coffee. It seems we have a mystery on our hands.'

I moved towards the coffee table—the only way I wanted to move because it brought me closer to the woman. Pete came over as well. We sat down and I lifted the heavy silver pot and poured into two bone china cups. There was no cream or sugar. The woman had a cup in front of her. I looked at her enquiringly. She shook her head. The tint of her skin, the slant of her eyes, the curve of her lips almost made me drop the pot.

'This is May Lin,' Sam said, 'my brother's daughter and therefore my niece. Her mother was a countrywoman of yours, Richard. May, this is Richard Browning and...'

'Peter McVey,' Pete rumbled. It was the only time I ever heard him call himself Peter; there was something about Sam's formality—the immaculate cream silk suit, smooth hair and precise language—that forced it out of him. Or maybe it was the woman—I'd have called myself Lord Browning, Earl of Newcastle on Hunter if I'd thought it would please her.

May Lin gave us a slight nod. She opened a beaded bag in her lap, took out a packet of Tareltons and lit one with a gold lighter. Did I say she was wearing a high-necked green silk dress, slit to mid-thigh? Well, she was. She blew smoke past me, seemed about to speak and then deferred to her uncle with her version of Sam's family head tilt.

'My niece has just had a most unpleasant experience,' Sam said.

Who is he? I thought. *I'll pound his head to jelly.*

'She has been working for Mr Hart Sallust as a secretary and script assistant. She hopes for a career in the movie business.'

Pete blurted, 'She should be in movies. She's beautiful enough.'

Sam's smile was quick and nervous. 'No, no. She aspires to be a writer and producer. There are problems.'

I knew what he meant. The old colour bar. Jimmie Wong Howe was a big noise cameraman, but I couldn't think of any other Chinese doing anything in Hollywood except bit parts. Look where they went when they wanted a Charlie Chan[8]. I lit a cigarette and May Lin pushed the ashtray slightly towards me. I smoked, drank coffee, tried to stop staring at every curve and fold of that green silk and listened to what Sam and May Lin had to say.

According to them, May Lin had been helping Sallust with his script and with his life. Sallust's most recent wife had left him a few months before and he needed taking care of.

'I knew him slightly,' May Lin said. 'We met again at a party and talked about writing and the business. I agreed to help him with the script. He agreed to share his credit with me if things worked out. It was a wonderful opportunity for me.'

'On the face of it, yes,' Sam said. 'But Mr Sallust is not a steady character. The work did not go well and he began to declare his love for my niece and to attempt to seduce her.'

That rang true. The helpless drunk, in need of a loving nurse, was one of Sallust's ploys. Watching May Lin as she smoked and put in a word here and there, I wondered at how Sallust could have had the nerve. Her skin was the colour of new ivory; her lips and fingernails were painted dark red and her hair was straight and glossy. But it was dark brown, not black and her eyes were green. The combination of characteristics made her devastating. I fought to control my breathing. I could hear McVey moving restlessly on his chair and I hoped that he wasn't going to pull out his notebook.

'So tonight we went out for a drive before beginning a long session on the script,' May said. 'Mr Sallust said the deadline was close and we might have to work straight through for a couple of days. He said he had some pills that would allow him to stay awake.'

'That'd be right,' I said.

'He was not going to drink. But it was no use. We went up to the Hollywood Lake. He had a bottle in the car and got very drunk. I had to drive and I don't like to drive such big cars. Then he wanted to go to the Trocadero. We went there but...'

'We know,' Pete growled. 'We were there tonight.'

'That is perhaps enough from us at this point,' Sam said. 'You mentioned Mr Sallust's name when you came in. Perhaps you would be good enough to state what business you have with him.'

Well, at that point, a matter of professional ethics entered the situation. I'd been happy enough to come straight to the point with Sung and I'd have told Sam everything he wanted to know if it'd been up to me. But this was different. It was McVey's case and I was just the hired hand. He had the say. I tore my eyes away from May Lin to look at Pete. He was chewing on a match, deep in thought. He reached into one of those cavernous pockets and took out his card. He slid it across to me. What else could I do? I got up and took it across to Sam's desk, thus demonstrating who was calling the plays on the McVey–Browning team.

'I can't see any harm in a little exchange of information, Mr Sam,' Pete rumbled. 'I've been hired to locate Mr Sallust, who's dropped out of sight. His... employer is worried. Mr Browning has been helping me.'

Sam's eyes rested on me briefly. 'Yes?' he said.

Pete spread his big farmboy hands. 'That's it. Now, perhaps you'd like to tell us where we can find Mr Sallust. I can see he behaved very badly towards Miss Lin. I'm here to tell you I'm going to dig him out and if he doesn't like it that's tough. He's in for a rough few days, so...'

'I don't believe you,' May Lin said.

I was so far gone I didn't believe him either momentarily, although I knew what Pete said was true.

'Now wait a minute. I've levelled with you.'

'That cannot be all,' May Lin said. 'He was not just drinking in the way some men drink. Weak men. He was frightened of something.'

'Yeah,' Pete said. 'He was later than the Second Coming with a piece of work he'd been contracted to do. I should guess he was scared.'

'Writers get something called a block,' I said. 'I'm not sure what it is, but I know they go on the sauce in a big way when it happens. I've seen it with Bill Faulkner and a few more.' I glanced at May Lin. 'They're often weak men as Miss Lin says. Maybe that's what was eating Hart.'

May Lin shook her head. She reached into her bag, took out a lace handkerchief and dabbed at her eyes. Then she undid the the collar of her dress and a couple of the fasteners below it. She pulled the green silk aside to show a sticking plaster at the base of her throat. The white plaster had some gauze under it and I could see a faint brown stain on the gauze. 'We were driving north from Malibu. Hart... Mr Sallust had the use of a house there and that's where we'd been working. I was driving slowly because I found the car difficult. We were stopped by a car cutting across us. Two men. One of them had a knife and he held it at my throat. The other one had a gun. They took Mr Sallust away with them.'

35

5

Well, you might say the story had more holes in it than a flyscreen and you'd be right. But at the time I bought it completely. She was such a wonderful looking woman I found it impossible to imagine that she wouldn't tell the absolute truth. And there were the tears and the blood on the bandage and Singapore Sam's obvious deep concern.

McVey shook his head. 'I dunno. Can you show us the house in Malibu? Can you show us where this happened? I suppose you reported it to the cops. Where are they? I don't see any buttons around.'

Sam's eyes glittered and he half rose from his chair. 'I am not used to having my word questioned,' he said softly. He looked at the card in his hand and then at me. 'You should tell Mr McVey that'

'He didn't mean anything,' I stammered. 'It's just...'

'I repeat,' Sam said, lowering himself back slowly and dropping the card on the desk, face down, 'that it is *you* who may be doubted. Can this be coincidence? A private detective is set on the trail of a man who is taken away at gunpoint. I hardly think so.'

I was confused now and nodded in agreement. 'That's right.'

'What's right?' McVey said.

I shrugged. 'There's something funny going on.'

'I do not call it funny,' Sam whispered. 'My niece has been assaulted, wounded. I cannot let this pass.'

It was pretty much of a standoff at that point. Sam didn't believe us and Pete didn't believe them. I could sense it in his movements. As for me, I *thought* Pete was on the level but I couldn't be sure, and I *wanted* to believe May Lin. We all sat there for a few minutes. My only worry was that Sam might call Big Sung in to do some persuading. Eventually May Lin said, 'Perhaps Mr McVey could talk to his principal. And his principal in turn might consent to give my uncle certain assurances.'

Pete took out a kitchen match and chewed the end of it. 'Maybe,' he said. 'That would be a fair-sized concession from our side. What's *your* contribution?'

'I could show you the house in Malibu and where the ... incident happened.'

That sounded fair enough to me but I couldn't see Sam agreeing to it. He closed his eyes and apparently went off into a meditation for a few minutes. He stayed perfectly still and appeared to stop breathing. When he opened his eyes again his brow was smooth and untroubled. 'Agreed,' he said. 'This can be done tomorrow.'

'Tomorrow!' Pete almost yelped. 'We've got a guy snatched. We can't wait till tomorrow. I can get ... my client on the line tonight and we can push it along.'

Sam held up his hand like a cop stopping traffic. 'My niece has had a severe shock. She cannot possibly do anything tonight. She needs rest. As you have heard, the men offered Mr Sallust no violence. He would not seem to be in immediate danger.'

May Lin seemed to remember that her dress was unfastened. She did it up slowly. I fancied she gave me a small smile. I know I was watching her like a man mesmerised. Pete examined his frayed match and dropped it into the ashtray which May Lin and I had half filled by this time. He looked at his watch and I did the same. It was a little past ten. Plenty of time to go after bad guys tonight, but Pete seemed to have something else on his mind. He stood up and gave May Lin a half bow, very courtly for Idaho. 'Could we say ten o'clock tomorrow morning?'

Sam said, 'I will expect you both and a telephone call from your client, Mr McVey, at that hour.'

'Fine,' Pete said. I stood up and nodded to Sam. I could hardly bear to look at May Lin in case I bumped into the furniture on the way out. I gave her a small wave and we left the room.

Nothing was said in the passage or in the room where the eating, drinking and music-playing was going on. I didn't see Big Sung. We collected our hats and went out to Pete's car. Pete settled himself behind the wheel and got out another match to chew. 'Well, that was a whole heap of cowshit.'

'What?'

'All of it,' he said. 'Or most.'

'I don't know,' I said, 'she'd been wounded. I could see the blood on the bandage.'

Pete snorted. 'Could've been ketchup. You see any on the dress?'

'No,' I admitted.

'Their story stinks. They're buying time to think up some more hokum. I just couldn't think of anything else to do in there, especially with that gorilla waiting in the wings.'

I was reluctant to accept this. 'It fits the facts. Sallust could've been hiding out in Malibu.'

'I said most of it was baloney. Why didn't they go to the cops after the girl got cut?'

'Well, that's easy. She wants to work in the movie business. You know how things are now, with the war on and all. Most people don't know the difference between Chinese and Japanese. Especially cops. A scandal like that would wipe her before she got a chance.'

Pete looked at me. 'She get to you, Rich? You fancy some of that yellow meat?'

I wanted to hit him. Love is blind, but not that blind. I said nothing. He pressed the starter and got the engine running. 'Get out,' he said.

'Why?'

'We're going to watch the place for an hour or six. You stay out here someplace and I'll watch the back. Anything happens you run around and let me know. Wave your hankie or something.'

I got out of the car and watched him cruise around to where he could make a turn and come back behind the club. I took up a position behind a hedge on the other side of the street and watched the front door. I knew enough not to smoke when on a stake-out like that, but the absence of tobacco made the minutes drag by like a tortoise with a broken leg. One hour felt like two, two hours felt like four. When the Packard drew up twenty feet away I was so stiff I could hardly move across the sidewalk. I clambered in, lit a Camel and sucked the smoke deep into my lungs.

'Didn't I tell you not to smoke in the car?'

I almost choked on the lungful. I got the window down and exhaled. I dragged again, blew the smoke out and dropped the cigarette into the gutter.

'Thanks,' Pete said. 'Nothing happened around back. I guess it was the same here?'

I nodded. 'I need coffee, tobacco and alcohol.'

'You're killing yourself, but it just so happens I've got a call to make at a place where there's a guy doing the same thing. You want to come along?'

I shrugged. 'Why not.' It was that or home and I knew that if I went home I'd drink and smoke too much and do nothing but think of ivory-tinted skin and slanted green eyes.

On the drive Pete added another detail. 'Why did the gorilla keep us waiting out in the hall?'

'I don't know.'

'To give them time to set up their story. The hell with it. We'll play along with them for a while. We've got no other leads, unless you've got something in mind.'

I shook my head.

'Didn't think so,' McVey said.

'So where are we going now?'

'Little something else I've got going on. Kinda weird. This guy's paying me a few bucks to talk to him.'

'What about?'

'Myself.'

He filled me in then on a short piece of his history he hadn't told me about before. He'd joined the army straight after Pearl Harbour and had seen some action in the Pacific. He'd been blown up by a grenade, suffered a head wound and had a silver plate in his skull holding it together.

'I get headaches,' he said. 'But I get a pension. So far it's a fair trade. In ten years' time I'll let you know. Anyway, I'm at the hospital a month ago, waiting to see a doc. Just routine. This guy's in the waiting room with me. Seems he brought his wife in for something or other. We get to talking. He tells me he was in the first war and got blown up. I tell him about the metal in my nut. I also tell him I'm a private detective. You never saw anyone so interested. Wants me to tell him all about it.'

I yawned. It looked like there was going to be a boring old vets' reunion coming up. Given my army record, deserted from the first war, invalided out of the second (and I have to admit there was a certain amount of malingering involved there), it wasn't exactly my sort of thing. 'About what?'

'About both. He wants to hear what it's like to have a plate in your head and how a private dick operates. Every time I go to see him he's got a list of questions. He pays me twenty bucks a session. That's useful dough.'

'Yeah,' I said. 'What's he do, this guy?'

'He's a writer. Name's Raymond Chandler. He writes a damn good book.'

The name didn't mean anything to me and the only use I had for books was for putting under short table legs. I yawned again and wanted a smoke. We turned into Drexel Avenue, south of Hollywood, and Pete pulled up outside a small ordinary-looking house. Not the kind of place you expect a writer to have. In my experience, writers either live in a pigsty or a palace. We went up the path to the front porch, which was in need of some work. It wasn't a bad neighbourhood, close to the Jewish stronghold on Fairfax Avenue. No view but not too much traffic.

Pete stabbed the buzzer. 'You'll like this guy if he's in a good mood.'

'What if he's not?'

'You'll hate him.'

A shortish, stocky man wearing a cardigan and carrying a cat answered the door. 'McVey,' he said. 'Do come in.'

We walked into a narrow hallway and along to a frowsy room with a lot of nondescript furniture and about a million books. McVey introduced us and I said, 'Glad to meet you.'

Chandler put his finger to his lips. 'Could you drop your voice a little. My wife's not well. She's sleeping.'

'Sorry.'

'That's all right. Well, I'm glad of the company. Can I get you a drink? I'm afraid I only have gin.'

'Gin's fine,' Pete said. 'Take a seat, Rich.'

Chandler put the cat down carefully on a pile of books where it balanced nicely. He brushed his cardigan down and tugged at the loosened ends of his bow tie. Then he adjusted his spectacles. 'Right,' he said, 'gin it is.'

McVey dropped into one of the big armchairs and I did the same. The room already smelled of tobacco smoke so I got out my Camels and added to the atmosphere. Pete chewed a match. Chandler came back carrying a tray with a gin bottle, some sliced limes, a bowl of ice, and three glasses on it. He had a pipe in his mouth and little wisps of smoke curled out as he spoke around the stem.

'Out of tonic, darn it.' He set the tray down on a table and made three solid gins with ice and lime. 'Happy days,' he said.

We all drank. I'd have been happier with whiskey but the gin was fine. I was glad he was out of tonic. Chandler sat back in his chair and took a tiny sip of his drink as if he intended to make it last a long time. He puffed his pipe and stared at the nearest bookshelf. 'I'm glad of the company,' he said. 'Writing's a lonely business.'

He had a peculiar voice, not quite American but a long way short of British. He looked about sixty; there was a lot of grey in his hair and his skin was pale. He seemed not to know what to do with his hands. They sort of drooped from his wrists and he fiddled with his glass and pipe and matches constantly. He was a very nervous fellow. From time to time he got up and peeked through a door into one of the bedrooms. Chandler and Pete got into a random conversation about war and wounds and, as the tobacco fog built up in the room and we worked our way through the gin, I almost nodded off. The cat wandered about the room and eventually settled on a cushion next to Chandler on the divan.

'Sleeping can be a problem,' I heard Pete say, 'but a few shots and an aspirin usually fixes it.'

'I suppose you have to watch out for blows on the head?' Chandler said.

'Yeah.' Pete laughed. 'But I'd watch out for that anyway. I been in this game a good few years and I never got hit on the head once. Not like the guy in your books.'

Chandler smiled and rambled on about punctuation and dramatic necessity. Something about the tone of his voice cut through the alcohol and tobacco fog. I stared at him, tried to imagine him different—younger, in uniform maybe. And then it came to me. I remembered when I'd met him before.

<u>6</u>

It was in France in 1918. I was in the Australian army and living in fear. They'd made me a sniper because I was a good shot. I thought it'd be a soft spot but it wasn't. The life expectancy of a sniper in France was measured in days, if not hours. I did as little as I could and deserted when things got too hot. On the last day of my military service, I was taking part in a British offensive, along with some Canadians and Kiwis, near Cambrai, south of Valenciennes. The bombardment was awful and men were dying around me like flies. The air was alive with flying metal and I dropped into a big shell hole to get out of it for a while. This Canadian sergeant was lying wounded in the hole, half-submerged in the mud. God, the memory of it makes me want a drink. The hole was full of corpses, British, German, Australian, all kinds.

Anyway, he told me his name—Ray Chandler—and that he was the only survivor of his platoon. They'd had a shell dropped on them or been blown up by a grenade, I forget which. He spoke with an English accent then and was thinner with more hair, but it was the same guy. He was interested to meet an Australian, but his manner was pretty high hat. I called a medic for him, I remember, and got the hell out of there. To stay in the one place[9] for more than a couple of minutes was asking for it.

Well, here we both were, in Hollywood, more than twenty years later and he was a writer and I was a detective, of sorts. Strange world. I took a closer look at him now and did some calculating. He couldn't have been sixty but he sure looked it, or even more. From the way he sipped his gin I guessed he'd gone a lot of rounds with the booze and had lost more than he'd won. At the moment he seemed to be holding his own. I didn't remind him of our meeting. It would have been too hard to account for my movements over the next few weeks and he looked like a shrewd old bird who could ask a good question. I just accepted some more gin and took a bit more interest in his conversation with Pete.

They talked about Pete's skull and about the private enquiry game and some of the cases Pete had handled. Pete talked pretty well. He was more modest than I'd have been if I'd handled some of those jobs—getting a rich kid off one of the gambling boats anchored off Santa Monica, finding the runaway daughter of an oil tycoon and arresting a San Quentin escapee who'd busted out specifically to kill Pete's client.

'My guy was as guilty as him, of course,' Pete said. 'But he'd had a better lawyer.'

'Law is where you buy it,' Chandler said and Pete nodded. I put in my two cents' worth from time to time but neither of them seemed very interested. I could have told them about the movie star and the sixteen-year-old triplets but somehow I thought they wouldn't have gone for it. All that talk about violence and yet they were both, at heart, quiet, bookish men. Chandler tried hard to be friendly, but there was something snooty about him that he just couldn't help. Weird.

'So, what's on your plate now, McVey?' Chandler said. He got himself another gin, only his third, but his voice was starting to slip a cog or two and it was a fair while since he'd looked in on his wife.

'Missing writer,' Pete said. 'Kind of strange case, Ray. You want to hear about it?'

'Night's young,' Chandler said.

It wasn't all that young. I asked where the bathroom was. Chandler gave me vague directions and I wandered off in search of it. There were books everywhere and too much furniture, some of it pretty good stuff. It looked as if the Chandlers had once had a bigger house and more money. They were still talking when I got back. I looked at the bookshelves and saw a bit of Chandler's own stuff—*The Big Sleep, Farewell, My Lovely, The High Window* in hardcover editions—as well as stacks of magazines like *Black Mask* and *Dime Detective* that carried some of his stories. It was hard to believe that this mild little guy could write about dames and death that way.

'The Chinese angle is interesting,' Chandler was saying. 'What d'you make of that, Browning?'

'Eh? Oh, nothing. I don't know. Beautiful woman. Is there much money in this writing game?'

'No. The money's in the movies. I've got an agent who's trying to get me some work with the studios.'

Don't do it, I thought, *they'll eat you alive.* 'Yeah. Hart Sallust seems to do all right. I think he's had a couple of Oscar nominations and that bumps up his price.'

Chandler winced as if this kind of talk was painful to him. He'd get a bellyful of it if he went to work in Hollywood. He puffed on his pipe, then pointed the wet stem at Pete. 'What questions have you been asking?'

Pete took out his notebook and rattled off a few things, like—why no blood on dress, why did the gorilla keep us waiting, why didn't they call the cops? How did she get back from Malibu? I was full of admiration, he was way ahead of me. But Chandler wasn't satisfied. He shook his head and poured himself another gin. He dropped in a slice of lime and watered it down with some of the melted ice.

'No, no. That's not what I mean. You're not asking the right question.'

'About what?' I said.

'About Sallust. If a rich man gets snatched what are they after?'

'His money,' I said.

'Right.' The pipe stem jabbed at me. 'If a diplomat or a spy gets kidnapped what's the motive?'

'Information,' Pete said.

'Just so. Now Sallust's a writer. Anything that happens to him probably has to do with his work. What's he writing at the moment?'

'I don't know,' Pete said.

'Appears to be giving him trouble, from what you say. Now there seem to be more than enough interested parties. Find out what he's writing about and you might get some idea of what's going on.'

Pete nodded. 'That's a great idea, Ray. Thanks.'

Chandler nodded. 'Welcome. Gentlemen, I think it's time to call it a night. Keep me informed, won't you?'

Pete said he would and accepted an envelope from Chandler as he showed us politely to the door.

On the way back to the Wilcox, Pete was thoughtful. I'd run out of smokes so there was no danger of me stinking up the car, also no danger of being thoughtful. I let my mind play on May Lin's shape under the silk dress, which doesn't require what you'd call thinking.

After a while Pete said, 'Strange bird, isn't he? Ray, I mean.'

That made me a little impatient. Just because I was slumped in the seat with my head back looking at the roof didn't mean I'd lost the plot. 'I know who you mean. Yeah, he is.'

'Do you know I've never seen his wife. She's always in bed. Wonder what's wrong with her?'

'Maybe he murdered her two years ago and he's just keeping up appearances.'

Pete glanced at me sharply. 'That ain't funny. Didn't take to him, uh?'

I said, 'He was all right.' But the truth was I had my reservations. Maybe it was the dim memory of how he'd ordered me about in that muddy hellhole. Maybe something else. Chandler reminded me of certain types I'd known at school—monitors, prefects, prize-winners; they carried a certain air of superiority even if you had six inches and twenty pounds on them [10] and were ordering them to fork over the pocket-money.

Suddenly, McVey swung the wheel. The car turned sharply right and my hat fell off. 'Hey. What're you doing?'

'We've got a tail,' Pete said. He drove carefully and smoothly, making occasional, natural-seeming turns until he was sure. I could see the lights in the rear-vision mirror and I was sure too. I wasn't worried; it would take a pretty good car to catch the finely-tuned Packard. I started to worry when I realised that Pete wasn't putting on the speed and he was heading for the canyons instead of the bright lights.

'Lose him,' I said. 'You can do it.'

'I don't wanna lose him. I wanna catch him.' Pete's voice lost its city smoothness when he got excited. In a shoot-out he probably snapped his braces and chewed tobacco.

'You don't know how much gun they've got.'

Pete patted the holster under his arm. I hadn't seen him put the gun back there, but people who're good with guns are like that. You never see the gun until it matters. 'I got enough,' he said. He grinned. 'Ray likes me to wear it.'

I pressed back against the seat. *Holy Christ*, I thought, *I'm in with one of those. He actually likes this stuff!*

We were almost to the foothills now and I was considering bailing out, but Pete chose that moment to increase speed.

'Hang on!'

We shot down a narrow, rutted road. Pete braked sharply and jumped out. I did the same in a pure reflex. 'What're we doing?'

Pete had his gun out and was pushing through the mesquite scrub towards the edge of the road we'd left. 'This is a dead end a hundred yards down. He won't be able to turn that Chevvy. We've got 'em!'

The moon was hidden by clouds and the night was pretty dark. No streetlights out there. I could see lights dotted around the canyons and hills where the people would be having their last sips of cognac before turning in. Smart people. I shoved my way up to the road and we began walking along in the fine white dust. I sneezed and Pete told me to shut up. I was sobering fast, the way I always have when danger is in the air.

'How do you know he won't be able to turn it?'

'Too narrow. Shut up and keep your eyes peeled. You got a gun?'

I did have, somewhere in my apartment. I hadn't seen it for months. I grunted and followed him, keeping as much of my body as I could in the shadows cast by the mesquite. I suppose Pete had in mind getting the drop on the guy in the Chevvy and getting him to spill his guts. Well, the best laid plans... The road bent and dropped in front of us and suddenly a set of headlights was blazing in our eyes and there was the roar of an engine at full throttle. I threw myself sideways, bounced off a tree trunk and crumpled down into the prickles and spines and rocks. Out of the corner of my eye I saw Pete's arm go up and I heard the sharp, snapping shots over the noise of the engine. Then all I could see was the night sky and all I could feel was cactus spikes in my butt.

Away to my left I heard Pete cursing. I struggled up out of my prickly bed and tried a few groans myself.

'You okay, Rich?'

'Yeah,' I said. 'What was that about him not being able to turn the car?'

McVey was up suddenly, rubbing his jaw. 'Goddamn branch got me.'

'Lucky you didn't hit your head, what with that plate in it and all.'

'Aw, I exaggerate that a bit for Ray. Well, I got one headlight. You see that?'

'Are you kidding? I was jumping for my life. I suppose you saw the driver and got the licence plate.'

'Missed the licence. There were two guys in the car. One of them looked like a Chink.'

'How could you tell? Those lights were blinding.'

'I was shading them to shoot. I saw him clear enough. Come on, I want to see how he did that. Some driver.'

We tramped down the slope and around the bend. The moon sailed clear of a cloud. Fifty yards ahead where the road ended a house was being built. Hundreds of tons of rock fill had been trucked in to provide a surface. They were going to hang a house off the canyon side the way they were doing all over the foothills.

'Goddamn it,' Pete said. 'I should've seen the marks of the trucks on the road. I'm losing my touch. At least I shot up that Chevvy some.'

7

At eleven o'clock the next morning things should have been a hell of a lot better. Pete McVey had gone off to search for a 1945 Chevrolet with bullet holes in it and I was driving towards Malibu with May Lin sitting next to me. She was wearing a red blouse with a high neck and a white sharkskin suit. Her hair was tied back with a scarf and she looked so good it was hard to keep my eyes on the road. It was a nice day too.

'Down here,' May Lin said.

I obeyed. I would have done anything she asked me, short of cutting my throat or giving up drinking. Maybe I'd even have given up drinking. The back road took us past some of the fancy beach houses to Paradise Cove, where the places ranged from clapboard shacks to brick villas. We pulled up behind a low, timber job that would have a beach frontage and just enough room between it and the houses on either side for you to squeeze past if you happened to be built like a breadstick. May Lin opened the door and stepped out of the car.

'No garage?' I said. I didn't fancy leaving the Olds on the street. The road was narrow and winding and anyone coming around the next bend too fast could easily side-swipe it. Repair shop bills were something I didn't need.

'We're not moving in,' she said.

You'll gather from that we hadn't been getting along as well as I'd hoped. When I picked her up at Sam's

I'd been freshly showered, shaved and cologned. I was wearing my lightweight suit and a newly laundered shirt. The sober, serious private detective, too tough for spats and pearl grey gloves, but looking his best. I might have been wearing bib overalls and Wellington boots for all the notice she took of me. By now, with the heat climbing, some of the gloss was coming off me. I'd loosened my tie and undone the top collar button. I got out of the car and peeled my jacket off. So what if sweat marks showed under my armpits. A healthy man sweats and shows it, especially if he's wearing a dark blue shirt. The hell with her. I lit a cigarette and crossed the road to where she was waiting by a gate in a brushwood fence.

As soon as I reached her I noticed the change in her manner.

'Could I have a cigarette?'

I gave her one and lit it. All very smooth, just showing a little resentment at the way I'd been treated. She blew the smoke over my shoulder, up, up and away towards the mountains where the moguls have their houses. They have swimming pools although they're less than a mile from the sea. I'm told the deer and coyotes like them.

'This house belongs to Akim Tamiroff,' May Lin said.

'I can't see him at the beach.'

'I don't think he ever came here but once. He said the light hurt his eyes.' She smiled. The first one today.

'I don't think he's ever played a daytime scene,' I said.

'My uncle tells me you're in pictures, Mr Browning.'

'Richard,' I said. 'Yes, I have been. In a small way. Not very exciting work, really.'

'You like excitement?'

Her green eyes were sparkling now and, through our cigarette smoke, I became aware of the special tang the Malibu air has, a matter of the mountains meeting the sea. This was a lot better. I gave her one of my manly grins and pushed at the gate. 'How are we going to get in here?'

Her hand came over mine and together we pushed the gate open. 'We left it unlocked last night. The house, too.'

I nodded. That was Hart. He never locked anything. He said that way things didn't get broken when redistribution of wealth took place. I think I know what he meant. We went through a large courtyard fringed with bamboos and banana trees to the small back porch. The house was nothing much—just a long, low structure built more of glass than of timber. I could see straight through it to the Pacific Ocean. The interior seemed to glow; it was a light and sun trap, more for the likes of Dorothy Lamour than Akim Tamiroff.

We went straight in through the back door. May Lin seemed to know her way around. She conducted me past the galley kitchen to the living room and through sliding glass doors on to the front deck. This jutted out until it almost overhung the sand. There was a short set of wooden steps, a hop, skip and a jump over some grass and then you had the stuff between your toes and were in funland. The waves crashed in heavily a bare seventy yards away.

'Nice place,' I said.

She nodded but didn't say anything. We crushed our cigarettes out simultaneously in the big sea-shell that sat on the rail of the deck. The shell looked as if it had been serving as an ashtray longer than it had as a home for a sea creature. I looked into those slanted green eyes with the heavy dark lashes and felt as if I was drowning. Maybe the beat of the waves on the sand helped the illusion. It happened very quickly. Our fingers touched as we butted the cigarettes, then our hands, then I had my arms around her and was crushing her against me and kissing her so hard I might have broken her neck if she hadn't been straining back against me, kissing fiercely and probing the inside of my mouth with her tongue.

After that, things galloped along. We ran to the nearest bedroom, ripped our clothes off and got down to business. She was lithe and active in bed, built and tuned up for a younger man, but I did my best and performed pretty creditably. The truth was, I didn't much care what happened as long as I could see and touch her and feel her hands on me and, as anyone who's spent any time in the sack knows, it's when you forget about yourself that you do your best work. When we'd finished she hunted around in my jacket for cigarettes and brought them back to bed. We lay smoking and touching and hardly talking at all. I might even have drifted off for a minute. Certainly I wasn't aware of her going away but when I next saw her she was standing beside the bed wearing her clothes and something of the old cool look.

'Well,' she said, 'aren't you going to search the house?'
'What?'

'I could tell that you and Mr McVey did not believe me. Now that you have satisfied your vanity you can check on my story.'

Well, May Lin was like that—a three-alarm fire one minute and an iceberg the next. I was so surprised that I did exactly what she said. After pulling on my shirt and trousers I padded through the house. There were a lot of books with Hart Sallust's name in them, some clothes that looked like they could have been his, a typewriter and several reams of paper. I took a look in the bathroom.

'No shaving gear,' I said.

'He wears a full beard.'

That was news to me but there was nothing unlikely about it. Writers grew and removed beards the way they went on and off the grog.

'Are you satisfied?'

Her manner and tone of voice cooled me right down. Normally, on a nice warm day in a beachhouse that had champagne in the fridge, I'd have been ready for another bout, but she was all business. Two could play at that. 'No,' I said, 'I'm not.'

'What do you mean?'

I pointed at the clean, tidy room that had served as a study. 'I never saw Sallust work in a room like that. He liked to work up to his knees in garbage—bottles, glasses, crumpled paper, books, magazines, cigarette packs, ashtrays...'

She said nothing.

'And another thing. Where's the work so far—the, what d'you call it—draft script?'

She smiled and shook her head. 'You don't understand. There was no draft script. There was nothing written. He could not write. That's why the study is the way it is. He would sit down at the typewriter and not even bother to roll in a sheet of paper.'

As I say, I'd heard of writer's block and had a vague idea of what it meant, but this sounded worse—like writer's blank. 'But you were supposed to be helping him, for how long?'

'Nearly three weeks.'

'What were you doing all that time? No, that's not the question. He must've talked about the script, the story at least. What was it about?'

I felt faintly ridiculous standing there in my shirt and pants and bare feet with her fully dressed and looking ready to go out to lunch. I also felt hungry and thirsty. And that was another of May Lin's great talents—she seemed to be able to read minds.

'Let's have something to eat and I'll try to explain. Why don't you get dressed, Richard? I've got a couple of calls to make.'

She used the phone in the study while I took a quick shower, dressed and opened a bottle of champagne. There was bread in the kitchen, cheese, tomatoes and cold cuts in the fridge. I loaded up a few plates and took them out to the deck. I'd gulped down one glass of champagne and was pouring another when she came out. She'd taken off her jacket and the scarf. Her long, brown mane fell over her shoulders. Her lipstick and nails were as red as her blouse and her eyes almost glittered in the bright sun. She gave me a smile before putting on a pair of sunglasses and accepting a glass of the bubbly. I began to feel encouraged. Still, the brief period of antagonism had reminded me that I was on a job. I felt proud that I'd hit on the right question and I asked it again.

She sipped her wine, cut a wedge of cheese and put it on a plate with a piece of bread. She looked at the food as if she just might eat it, if it was lucky. 'Do you know much about writing for the movies, Richard?'

I shook my head and swallowed a mouthful of meat, bread and pickle. 'Nothing.'

'Most of it takes place in the head. The writer has a storyline, characters. He imagines the scenes and hears the dialogue. He writes it down, builds up the characters and develops the story as he goes along. Sometimes the characters change and the story goes in unexpected directions. There are no rules except that you need three acts, like a play.'

I nodded and kept eating. The champagne was good but it was going to warm quickly out in the sun. I poured another glass.

'Mr Sallust had a peculiar assignment for this picture. He agreed to write a movie for John Garfield. He didn't tell them what his story idea was and they didn't ask.'

'I never heard of that,' I said. 'Usually the studio buys a story. Then they buy a writer.'

'Mr Sallust is a close friend of the producer, Joe Herman. They worked out an arrangement whereby Mr Sallust needed to inform Mr Herman about the progress of the script only in the most general terms—the number of characters, foreign and domestic locations, set requirements, that sort of thing. Mr Sallust said it was a breakthrough—the first time a screenwriter had worked with the sort of freedom a novelist has.'

'Sounds bloody dangerous to me,' I said. 'What if he came up with something like a tightrope walk across Niagara Falls or a plane flight under the Sydney Harbour Bridge[11]?'

'Under the what?'

'Never mind. Go on.'

She drank some wine but still didn't touch the food. The edge of the piece of meat was curling. 'It was risky, yes. But Mr Sallust had Herman's confidence. Unfortunately, things did not go well.'

I was feeling a little drowsy by this time. Who wouldn't after sex, wine and sun? There was a scattering of people on the beach and a few in the water although the day wasn't really hot. I got to thinking of Stockton beach, near Newcastle, and the Sydney beaches where I'd swum a fair bit before the war, the Great War, that is. Those were the days—long, clear, hot Australian summers and the deep green Pacific Ocean as cool and clean as...

'Richard! Are you listening?'

'Eh? Yes, yes, of course. John Garfield and no bloody story. Go on.'

I thought I'd recovered pretty well but I was wrong. She was offended by me going off into a brown study. She tossed off her wine. 'What's the use? You're not interested and too stupid to understand. This is a waste of time.'

'Hey, come on now. I'm sorry. Have a bite to eat...'

'You are a fool. I want to go.'

'Not until you tell me what Sallust was writing.'

'I don't know! Nothing. He was drunk most of the time. He talked a bit about some characters, he didn't even have names for them. There was no story. Just ideas. Boy meets girl, boy can't have girl. Nonsense like that.'

'I get it,' I said. 'He was in love with you and he couldn't get his head straight to write anything because you wouldn't...'

She'd been staring out at the water. Now her head jerked around. 'That surprises you, doesn't it? That I wouldn't. Well, you're right. I wasn't attracted to him and I don't sleep with men I'm not attracted to.'

That sort of remark was what I was waiting to hear. I put down my glass and reached across the table for her hand. 'Don't be cross, May. I believe you. I think we should go inside and...'

'No. I want to go back to the city. I want to forget all about this. Please take me back.'

What could I do? I had the answer to the question Pete was sure to put to me. Not much of an answer but at least I could show I'd been on the ball. And although I was powerfully attracted to May Lin, these swings of mood were sure to prove wearing over the long haul. So it was back to business. I finished off the champagne and threw the food out onto the grass. A circling flock of seagulls swooped and started fighting over the titbits. The biggest, fattest ones got the lion's share as they always will. 'Right,' I said. 'We'll go back, but first you'll show me where the alleged kidnap took place.'

There I was again, asking the right questions. Pete McVey and Raymond Chandler would have been proud of me.

8

It was hot in the car, even with the windows down. The sky had taken on a grey-blue sullen look the way it can in LA and there was no breeze either from the mountains or the sea. Hot and still, like a summer day in Melbourne. I found myself remembering the old days in Australia more and more as the years went by. Things were simpler then—have a good time today and tomorrow and don't worry about next week pretty well summed it up. I drove along the road towards the Ventura County line. It was even hotter here. The only cool thing around was May Lin's disposition.

'What the hell were you doing out here?' I said. 'We're on the way to Santa Barbara, for Christ's sake.'

'He said he wanted to drive.'

We drove. The road narrowed and we were really in the sticks—canyons off to the right and rugged coastal country on the other side. They tell me some of the stars have their houses there now, out as far as the Yerba Buena Road. In 1943 the only things living there ran around on four legs or had wings. I was getting suspicious, but May Lin was such a mysterious creature you could get suspicious about the way she smoked a cigarette. I looked at the speedometer and resolved to give it another mile, two at the most.

The road dipped and swung west and I had a view of the sea that took my breath away. The oil derricks might be at work a few miles further north, but here the water was as deep and blue and untroubled as in Columbus's time. The coastline was rocky with small beaches tucked away in pockets. Very romantic. I glanced across at May Lin but she was looking in the other direction, at the brush beside the road and the cottonwood trees beyond that. I should have been more suspicious—that sea view was a knockout, but the beauty of it took my attention and wiped my brain pan clear of thought.

The big black car came up out of nowhere. I heard a siren and pulled over and slowed down like an honest citizen. The next thing I knew two men with hats pulled down over their eyes and sunglasses on above their tough expressions were pulling open the front doors of my car. I heard May Lin scream and I saw a gun. I knew what to do and I was scared enough to do it. I reached for the gun in my jacket pocket, the one I'd located and cleaned and filled with bullets last night. I jerked it clear of the pocket smoothly and aimed somewhere above the head of the man who was reaching behind his back for something. I pulled the trigger once, twice. There were little dry snaps, no satisfying, scary booms. I swore and then I heard a swishing sound and the blue sky turned black and the hot air turned cold and the sagebrush beside the road didn't have any smell at all.

When I returned to the land of the living my trousers were down around my knees because my belt was around my ankles. My wrists were behind my back, strapped tight, and, since my tie was missing, I concluded that it was doing the job. I was lying on the floor of a cabin—rough pine walls, unlined roof, Indian rug over the deal boards. There was a stone fireplace and some solid, amateur-built furniture. My head ached and the taste in my mouth made me think I'd been chewing on the rug. I hadn't, but I'd been dribbling on it some. I wriggled around trying to get a better look at the place. One room—wood stove, tap and enamel sink, storage shelves with cans and packets on them. There was a folding cot with some army issue blankets on it under the small window. Not the Ritz.

The light was dim in the cabin and looked to be fading outside. That made it late in the afternoon. Say, five hours since I'd been knocked out. A feeling of panic swept over me. What if I had a fractured skull? I'd been knocked out a couple of times before—once when I was trying to jump on board a freight train and again in a boxing ring when we were filming a turkey called *The Leather Pushers* and I moved my head to the right instead of the left. The first time I woke up in Mexico and the second [12] I needed bridgework. I did what I could to check on my state of health—blinked my eyes, ran my tongue around my mouth and checked for dried blood from my nose or ears. I must have looked like an idiot with a half dozen facial tics. There was no serious damage as far as I could tell. That left me free to worry about the big picture—who'd done this to me and what would they do next?

My next thought was for May Lin. I'd heard her scream when the guys with the guns got to work but that didn't necessarily mean anything. Anyone can scream. I could have screamed myself right there and then and don't think I didn't feel like it. What made me sceptical about May Lin's screaming was the gun. I knew I'd checked and loaded it and that it was in good working order when I'd put it in my pocket. When I'd needed it the gun had been about as useful as a toothbrush. And who'd fossicked in my pockets for cigarettes and got herself showered and cleaned up while I'd snatched forty post-lovemaking winks?

That was more than enough thinking. The thing to do was to get free. I spent ten minutes or so rolling about on the floor, trying to work loose the belt and the tie. No luck. Then I rolled around some more in an effort to find something I could use to do some cutting—a wood axe, a fire iron, a bed spring, a dustpan. Nothing. I got even closer to screaming point, or weeping point. It could have gone either way. Then I heard footsteps outside the cabin door and voices. I rolled back to approximately the point I'd started from and lay doggo.

The door opened.

'Jiminy Crickets, Mr Brown. I cleaned this place up. I swear I did and lookit now.'

'It sure is a mess, Hank.'

'He's trussed up like a Thanksgiving turkey. I can't see how...'

Mr Brown touched my ribs with the toe of his right wingtip. 'That's because you just plain don't know enough about this business, Hank. Now, me, I was in the marines a spell, and when we wanted a man tied up good, why, we'd just run a line to his neck so that if he moved he throttled himself. See? A gentleman tied up like that got the message real quick.'

I sneaked a look at Hank and Mr Brown through slitted eyes. Hank was a string bean in denims, flannel shirt and work boots. He had a rifle slung across his shoulder. Mr Brown was a smooth, citified number in a cream linen suit with a waistcoat which was unusual in LA about then. He was recently barbered and he had very white teeth. He could've been an actor except that he was carrying a little too much weight for a youngish man. His dark straight hair was slicked back and shiny. He was frowning and his eyes were hooded. His shirt was as white as his teeth. He wore some kind of gold bracelet that hung down below his French cuffs. There was no gun in evidence, but of the two men, he was the one I was most afraid of.

He leaned down, grabbed me by the shoulders and lifted me into a chair. I weighed about a hundred and ninety at the time. Some lift. Then he reached up to a shelf and took down my wallet, pistol and other odds and ends that had been in my pocket. 'Put some coffee on the stove, Hank. Me and this Jasper's going to have a little talk.'

I didn't want coffee. I didn't want anything except to be out of there. Brown flicked through the wallet. 'Browning, eh? Detective, eh?'

'Not really,' I said. 'I'm an actor, resting between jobs, actually.'

'Shut up!' He slapped me across the face with the leather wallet. Good quality leather. It hurt. My head started to ache in another place. That made at least four. I could hear Hank rattling cups and pots and running water into the sink. Suddenly my mouth was dry and I couldn't tell whether it was fear or thirst or both. It's remarkable how you keep thinking, even when your life is in danger. I realised that neither Hank nor Brown had been on the road near the Ventura County line. Meaning there were more than four men in on this little game, whatever it was. When was that? It seemed like days ago but it was only hours. I was thinking, but not thinking straight. Best to say as little as I could. Hank brought Brown a mug of coffee and he sipped at it while he looked at my possessions.

'Cheap wallet. Cheap gun. Cheap business. You're over your head, cheapie.'

No point in arguing. The wallet had cost the girl who had the second lead in *The Desert Song* twenty-five bucks. My voice was a croak. 'How about some coffee? I'm mighty dry.'

Brown let out a bellow of laughter. 'Reckon you might be an actor at that. "I'm mighty dry." I don't reckon I've ever heard anyone say that outside the movies. Have you, Hank?'

Hank wasn't as dumb as he looked. He smirked and let his twangy voice go slow and droopy, like Gary Cooper's, 'Nope.'

That got another laugh from Brown. I tried a grin but got smacked in the face again for my pains. 'This isn't funny, cheapie. This isn't the movies. What's your interest in Hart Sallust?'

I was almost glad to be back on the subject again. 'Hired to find him,' I said. 'By his agent... script's due... Garfield movie...' The lack of interest on Brown's smooth face was making me nervous and breaking up my train of thought. *Christ, what can I tell him?* I thought. *What does he want to hear?*

'We don't believe that,' Brown said.

'We?' I yelped. 'Who's we? It's the truth!'

Brown shook his head. 'I don't think so. Too much of a coincidence and we don't believe in coincidences.' He sighed. 'Too bad.'

'What?' I said. 'What's too bad?'

He drank some of his coffee, shuddered and put the mug down. I noticed then the big gold signet ring on his right hand and how it brought out the brownness of his skin. The dark hair was very dark and the hooded eyes were slightly slanted. Mr Brown had quite a bit of the Asian in him and the fact didn't comfort me one bit.

'Water,' I said.

He slapped me with the wallet again.

I sucked the blood from my lips. 'Where's May Lin?'

He raised his hand to hit me again and then thought better of it. 'Hank,' he said, 'go outside and look around. Make sure no-one's taking an interest.'

'Ain't no-one around for half a mile,' Hank whined. 'Waste of time.'

'Just do it.'

Hank hesitated. I could see he didn't like taking orders from a man who wasn't white, especially when he, Hank, had a gun to hand. *Maybe he doesn't like seeing a white man being beaten up by a Chink*, I thought.

But that was clutching at straws. Hank swilled down his coffee, shouldered his rifle and went outside.

'Okay, Mr Detective,' Brown said, 'time for a little private chat. Let me tell you what I've got in mind. I'm going to ask you a question. If I get a good, straight answer I'll ask you another one.'

That didn't sound so hard. 'What if you don't?' I said.

He reached into the pocket of his immaculately draped cream suit and took out a small pair of pliers. 'In that case. I'll pull out one of your fingernails. I guess I can spin it out to ten questions, give or take a couple.'

The pliers fascinated me. They had narrow jaws and red rubber grips. They were the cruellest-looking things I'd ever seen and I could feel my bladder getting ready to let go. 'You have to believe me,' I stammered. 'I've told you the truth. I was hired to find Sallust because...'

'Who hired you?'

I thought that over. It wasn't a situation you wanted to name names in, but I had no choice. 'Robert Silkstein. The agent.'

He clicked the pliers. 'When?'

'Couple of days ago.'

He stood up and for one ghastly minute I thought he was going to circle around behind me and go to work, but he moved over to the window. I swivelled my head to see him. He rubbed dust off the pane and looked out. It was dark outside now and all of a sudden I felt the air temperature in the cabin drop. It would be a damn cold place at night, even in spring. God knows why I was noting these things, they weren't likely to do me a blind bit of good. Brown left the window, moved up behind me and grabbed my right hand. I screamed as I felt the pliers bite my flesh and click shut.

Brown laughed. He came around and showed me what he'd done. He'd pushed the pliers onto my right thumbnail, forcing back the top of the thumb, and nipped out a half-inch-square section of the nail. He held it under my nose. My thumb was on fire and I retched. Nothing came up except a nasty noise and a sour smell because my stomach was empty. 'Once again. Who hired you?'

I had to say something different. I didn't want to but a man can only take so much. 'A private detective named Pete McVey from Santa Barbara. He told me Silverstein hired him, like I've told you. That's all I know. I swear it's true. Jesus, don't come near me with those...'

Brown opened the pliers and let the piece of nail fall into my lap. He'd done a bit of ripping to get it free. There was blood on it. I almost fainted at the sight. Then I heard Hank's voice from the door.

'No-one around, Mr Brown. How tough is he?'

'Not very,' Brown said. 'The trouble is, I think he's telling the truth.'

'I am. I swear.'

'I don't think it's going to do you any good, cheapie, but I need instruction on this.'

'Wh-what d'you mean, instruction?'

'Never mind. Are you a religious man, Browning?'

'No.'

'Pity. Hank's religious, aren't you, Hank?'

'God-fearing, anti-Communist Christian. That's me,' Hank said.

Brown smiled and slipped the pliers back into his pocket. I was never so relieved to see a man do anything in my life. 'Salt of the earth, that's our Henry. Where's the nearest phone, Hank?'

'Garage back down the road a ways. 'Bout a hundred yards from the highway. Name of Art...'

Brown raised the finger with the signet ring on it to his lips. 'Ah, ah, no names. Not that it'll matter much, I expect. Keep an eye on Mr Browning while I go and make a call. You might encourage him to say some prayers. Maybe you know some you could teach him.'

'I know some,' Hank said.

'Splendid. I won't be long. I'll take the Plymouth.'

Brown left the cabin and I looked at Hank. He gave me a brown-toothed grin and settled himself on the edge of the table. His rifle lay across his lap. Hopeless weapon and position for shooting at close range, but quite okay if your target is tied hand and foot.

'I could do with a drink,' I said.

'I don't touch liquor, mister.'

'I meant water.'

He came over and checked my hands and feet, taking care to keep clear of a kick or any other sudden movement. He needn't have worried—I was numb everywhere.

'Can't see the harm,' he said. He went to the sink and ran water into a glass. He brought it back and held it to my mouth. I drank gratefully. The water got rid of the foul taste in my mouth. I nodded my head for more, considered spitting it at him, but what would be the point? I closed my eyes and let the water go down my throat. *Dignity*, I thought, *die with dignity.*

'You want to say a prayer?'

'No. I just don't want to die ignorant. What's this all about?'

Hank resumed his position at the table. He scratched his stubbled chin and looked at a point somewhere above my head. 'I can't rightly say. I just know we've got to fight those commies, here and now.'

'Russians?' I said. 'I've got nothing to do with any Russians.'

He shook his head. 'Chinks. Chink commies. Can you imagine it? Five hundred million commie Chinks? Can you imagine what that would mean to Christian America?'

I couldn't. 'No,' I said. 'And I can't see what it's got to do with me. Listen Hank, this Brown, he's a bit of a Chinaman himself. Maybe he...'

'Shuddup!' Hank raised the rifle and pointed it at me. I closed my eyes and heard the shots, the booms bouncing off the walls of the tiny cabin.

9

As the smoke cleared and I discovered that I was still alive, I pieced together what had happened. Pete McVey had kicked the door in, Hank had fired a shot at him which missed and Pete had shot Hank between the eyes. The scrawny man lay on the Indian rug; his thin, bitter face was obliterated above the cheekbones by blood welling out of the wound and spreading. There was a dark, grey puddle under his head. I choked on the gunsmoke and coughed. Pete was standing shocked in the doorway with his big pistol pointing in my direction.

'Hey, Pete,' I said, spluttering, 'point that thing somewhere else. Boy, am I glad to see you. Help me get untied. I'm losing circulation in my arms and legs.'

He moved across the room, tucking his pistol away in his jacket and glancing down at Hank. By the time he'd reached me he'd regained his composure.

'Damn fool shouldn't have fired,' he said. 'Didn't have a chance.'

I nodded. 'That's right. Got a knife?'

He produced a clasp knife and cut through my tie. Then he bent to saw through the belt but I stopped him. 'Hold on. That's a good belt. I can unbuckle it.'

Pete folded the knife. 'You're a cool one, Rich.'

There's nothing I like better than admiration from a man of action, unless it's admiration from a woman of action. I took a quick look at Pete, judged he hadn't heard me give his name to Brown, and held up my mangled thumbnail. 'They'd made a start,' I said. 'Hank here was a Christian wowser[13] if ever I met one, but do you think there'd be a drink in the place?'

While Pete fossicked in the cupboards I got the belt undone and put it back on my pants. That allowed me to pull my pants up and restore a little dignity. I massaged my arms and legs and didn't try to stand just yet. No sense in surrendering the sympathy vote too early. McVey produced a bottle of brandy and poured two hefty slugs into enamel mugs. I took a good pull on mine, sank it in a second gulp and held out the mug for more.

'Easy,' Pete said. 'You'd be in shock, I guess.'

'Best thing for it. How the hell did you get here? Hey, what about the other guy? He could be back any moment. Gimme that rifle...'

'I saw him go. What was he doing?'

'Going to make a phone call to see if he should shoot me or cut my throat.'

'It's a half-hour round trip. We've got some time. We can get him when he comes back.'

I liked that. I liked the idea of having Mr Brown in the sights of Hank's Winchester. As I worked my way through some more brandy I listened while Pete filled me in on how he'd happened to turn up in the right place at the right time. He admitted that he'd lied when he'd said he hadn't got the licence number of the car that nearly ran us down. He'd got enough of it to run a trace and locate its registered owner in Santa Monica—Charles Tan. He'd gone out there and chanced upon the Chevrolet, bullet holes and all, heading in the direction of Malibu and parts north. The Chevvy reconnoitred the cabin then pulled off the highway a few miles south of the Ventura County line.

'Hot out there waiting, I can tell you,' Pete said.

'Do you mean to tell me you were there when they stopped May Lin and me? When they sapped me? You just sat there?'

'Now hold on there buddy. All happened so fast. And I wasn't exactly on the spot. Mr Tan and his Chevvy...'

'What happened to May Lin?' I said urgently. 'Pete, was she hurt? Did they rough her up? Or was she in on it with them?'

McVey rubbed his big jaw and looked at his watch. 'Rich, I can't say for sure. I was up the road a ways. Hadn't we better get ready for this guy, what d'you call him?'

'Brown.'

'Big, smooth-looking hombre in a cream suit?'

'That's him.'

'Charles Tan, according to the motor licence department.'

I had my circulation back now, and my confidence, boosted by the brandy. Hank's smashed head didn't worry me now. If he was right, he was with his God in heaven; if he was wrong, and I was pretty sure he was, what the hell did it matter anyway? I stepped over him, picked up the Winchester and put a shell into the chamber.

'Looks like you know what you're doing,' Pete said.

'I was a sniper in...'

'Spain?'

I grunted. 'Doesn't matter. Let's see what Mr Brown or Mr Tan has to say when he gets back. He's got this pair of pliers in his pocket. I might put them on one of his teeth and see if it gets him talking.'

'Easy, Rich. I agree we should take him but we've got some problems here. I mean, a dead man?'

'Self-defence,' I said

Pete checked his pistol and shook his head. 'What county're we in? What's the law out here?'

'I don't know.'

'Makes a difference.'

He was right. Those parts of the Hollywood/LA complex that fell under county policing were run differently from the parts that were incorporated into the City. Both were as corrupt as Nero's Rome, but you could buy more law for less money in the counties than in the city. 'We'll worry about that later,' I said. 'Brown said he was driving a Plymouth.'

Pete nodded. 'Two-tone job, maroon and blue.'

'You wait in here,' I said, suddenly very much in charge. Maybe it was the brandy, maybe the thumbnail, maybe the Winchester. 'I'll brace him outside.'

'Don't shoot him, Rich,' Pete said. 'We don't know shit about what's going on.'

I checked the rifle. One in the chamber and eight in the magazine, .44 calibre, lever action, well greased. 'I won't hit him anywhere that matters,' I said.

Charles Tan, aka Mr Brown, didn't show. Pete and I waited for over an hour. Then we scouted around the cabin for a time. Nothing happened. I got my first good look at where I'd been taken against my will, interrogated and tortured. It was a nice, modest little place on a canyon road with another running past a mile or so above it and the lights of the highway just visible away to the west. We searched the cabin thoroughly but found nothing to suggest that it wasn't just what it seemed—somebody's holiday shack, a place for walks, chopping wood and cooking flapjacks.

'Door was forced,' Pete said, examining the jamb. 'I'd say our boys just picked out a handy cabin for a couple of hours.'

I was busy collecting my belongings, stuffing the bits of necktie in my pocket and wiping down surfaces. Hank was starting to look even deader.

'What're you doing?' McVey said.

'Cleaning up.' I tried to think of all the things that bring people in these situations unstuck. I found the bloody bit of thumbnail and wrapped it in my handkerchief along with the butts of the seven cigarettes I'd smoked since getting free. *The casing from the bullet Pete had fired? No, the gun's a revolver. No casing ejected.* I took the enamel mugs over to the tap and rinsed them.

'You planning to just walk away from this?'

'What else can we do?' I said. 'Let's see, we'll have to brush out the tyre marks or drive over them a few times. Where's my lighter?'

'In your hand.'

I looked around the cabin, avoiding the upturned face of Hank. 'Where's my hat?'

'Last I saw, it was beside the highway. Probably blown into the brush by now.'

'Have to get it,' I said. 'I think that'll about do it.'

Pete lit a cigarette and picked up a metal ashtray. I wanted to tell him to be careful of prints but something about the way he looked at me kept me quiet. 'Great,' he said. 'Nice you got everything tidied up. Now I can ring the Santa Monica cops. Thinking about it, I reckon they'd be the boys to handle this.'

'Are you crazy? There's a dead man here. You shot him.'

Pete blew smoke and pointed to a mark above the doorway. 'Should be a 30-30 bullet in there. And I've got a witness it was self-defence.'

I looked at the rifle lying on the table. My prints were all over it and I would've forgotten them. If Pete was going to stay and claim self-defence, how would he explain a rifle wiped clean of prints? Answer, he couldn't and didn't intend to. I considered skipping out and leaving him to it, but a number of things stopped me. One, he'd saved my life. Two, I wanted to know what had happened to May Lin and, three, Charles Tan and his mates were still out there somewhere, still threatening. Pete McVey was a good ally. I put on a grin I didn't feel and sat down on the torture chair. 'I was just kidding, Pete. What're the Santa Monica cops like?'

'Lousy,' Pete said. He put his hat on and stubbed out his cigarette. 'Get ready, Rich. You're in for another bad time.'

He was right. Pete McVey had an annoying habit of being right. Detective Lieutenant Burt Martingdale and his offsider, Sergeant Hamer, were almost as unpleasant as Charles Tan and Hank. Neither they nor the two uniformed men whose names I didn't catch who arrived first, expressed any regret about Hank. Cops are like that. They see too many corpses to care and what they really like is kicking living heads. I had the impression that Martingdale and Hamer were past masters, when they felt like taking the trouble. They sneered at Pete's licence and credentials only slightly less than they sneered at mine.

'Torture?' Martingdale said after I'd shown him the bit of thumbnail. 'I do worse than that to myself with my teeth when I'm tense.'

'I can't imagine you being tense, Lieutenant,' I said. 'I like the way you step across a dead body.'

Martingdale had done that, showily, a few times. Now he swivelled and punched me in the stomach hard enough to bend me over. 'Oh, sorry Mr Browning. My fist slipped...'

Pete McVey growled and Hamer grinned at him. 'Something on your mind, peeper?'

'Yeah,' Pete said. 'We've told you what happened here, as much as we can...'

'You've told us shit,' Martingdale said. 'You're looking for someone you won't name. Some guys you don't know snatched Browning and brought him here.'

'And tortured me,' I said.

'Yeah,' Hamer said. 'And you said nothin'. I can see you got hero written all over you.'

'At least I've got my army discharge papers,' I said. 'Like Mr McVey...' I let the implied insult hang in the air.

Martingdale turned on me savagely. 'Listen, you limey son of a bitch. I don't care if you swam back from Dunkirk. This is Los Angeles county, nineteen-forty fucking three and you're a couple of hairs in my nose. There's nothing in this for me. You won't tell me who you're working for or what it's all about. All I've got is one dead cracker and a couple of smart peepers who can make a self-defence case. It was hardly worth getting out of bed for. Might as well be a nigger cutting for all the juice in it.'

Martingdale was a big, handsome man, running to fat but still with a few years of appeal for the women left in him. It didn't surprise me that he'd been in the sack that early in the evening. It would have surprised me if the partner had been his wife. Hamer was small and rat-faced with thin, mousey hair. I sensed that he hated Martingdale's guts but was smart enough never to show it. Martingdale wasn't smart enough to see it.

'I dunno, Lieutenant,' Hamer said, 'this stiff looks kinda familiar to me. Maybe we better hold these two a while, till we find out who he is.'

Martingdale sneered. 'You figure he's the governor's brother, out shooting coon. Something like that?'

Hamer was used to the sarcasm and didn't let it faze him. 'Hell, we don't even know who the cabin belongs to.'

'Neither do we,' I said.

'Who asked you?' Hamer snarled. 'It just sticks in my craw to let these birds go.'

'You'd be wasting your time to do anything else,' Pete said. 'Our lawyers'd have us out in the morning and all you'd have would be ink on your fingers.'

All very well for you, I thought. *I don't have a lawyer.* I stayed well clear of the breed—I suspected that they communicated among themselves and there were a few things in my past, matters pending, you might say, I didn't want anyone to pick up on. Still, I nodded and tried to look as if I had a fancy mouthpiece, too. Hamer examined me closely.

'Where have I seen you before?'

'*Kid Galahad? Sante Fe Trail?*' I said.

'Jesus,' Martingdale growled. 'A play-actor. Probably both pansies.'

Pete turned red and his right fist bunched, but he didn't say anything. Martingdale heaved his body off the table, where he'd arranged himself in a pose that would've looked better when he was twenty pounds lighter. 'We've got your names and addresses. We'll take the Colt.' He pointed to Pete's gun which was on a chair beside the body. 'Anything to add?'

Pete and I shook our heads.

'Right. You have a word with your lawyers and the client and be at my office tomorrow at three. If you don't show up and if you haven't got a better story, you can tear those licences up and put them down the john. Let's go, Hamer.'

He took a manila envelope from his pocket, scribbled on it and dropped it on the chair next to the Colt; he signalled to the uniformed men to do something about the gun and the body and stalked out of the cabin. Hamer gave us one brief, malevolent glance and followed him.

I gave Pete a cigarette and lit us both up. 'I'm glad you've got a good lawyer,' I said. 'This is a ticklish spot.'

Pete watched a cop push his gun into the envelope using a pencil. 'I haven't got a lawyer,' he said.

10

On the drive back to LA I smoked all my cigarettes and some of Pete's. I'd taken the brandy from the cabin and used a bit of that too. I forgot about my hat but suddenly I remembered my car.

'Hey, my car?'

'They took it,' Pete said. 'Last I saw it was heading back to the city. It'll turn up.'

'It better,' I said. 'I still owe money on it. Where the hell are we with this thing, Pete?'

Instead of answering, McVey questioned me carefully about the time I'd spent with May Lin. I told him all I could remember which, despite the booze and the sapping and the torture, was just about everything. I've got a memory that seems to be protected from all the painful, damaging things that happen to me. As I was talking, I realised that it didn't add up to much.

'At least we can go after Charles Tan,' I said.

Pete flipped his empty Luckies pack out the window. 'I doubt it. I still can't work out how he knew not to come back to the cabin. Still, he's a pretty smart customer. He'll calculate you're on the loose. Maybe the papers'll carry something about Hank tomorrow. That Hamer looked like a boy to make a buck from the reporters, wouldn't you say?'

'Could be. What're you saying?'

'Charles Tan'll disappear. There's one detail you might be able to fill in, Rich?'

I was sucking at the mangled fingernail, trying to stop it throbbing. 'Shoot.'

'May Lin. You figure she set you up?'

'I don't know. Wait, I'll check my gun.' I'd taken the .38 down from the shelf where Brown/Tan had put it. The cops hadn't frisked me. I ejected the magazine and checked the action. There was a bullet wedged in the breech. 'Jammed,' I said. 'Hard to say. Might've just happened...'

'You were in the sack with her, right?'

'Sure, but that doesn't...'

'What I mean, dummy, is did you take a look at that bandage on her neck? Was she still wearing it?'

'Jesus, I don't remember.'

'Come on. You didn't do it with your clothes on, did you?'

I tried to remember but I couldn't. Had there been some kind of a bandage, a sticking plaster? Had she worn a ribbon or a scarf? I didn't think so, but I just couldn't get a clear picture. I shook my head. 'Nothing. Maybe the crack on the head scrambled the memory.'

'Guy doesn't usually forget things like that,' Pete complained. 'Okay, tell me again about Hank and the commies.'

I ran through what I remembered of Hank's rambling about Christianity and Communism. None of it made any sense to me and I said so.

Hank grunted. We were getting close to Santa Monica, to the place called the Gold Coast where the stars used to live before the action shifted north to Malibu. We'd have to turn off here tomorrow and report to the cops if Pete was planning to play it that way. He had to concentrate on his driving now that the traffic was heavier. We were heading towards downtown LA before he spoke again. 'Know much about what's happening in China around now, Rich?'

'Nothing,' I said.

'Don't keep up with the foreign news, eh?'

'Where I come from people used to worry about China all the time. They reckoned the Chinese were going to come down and take over Australia. That's why they sent them all back after the gold rush and wouldn't take in any more.'

'That's interesting,' Pete said.

'Not if you heard about the yellow peril morning, noon and night, the way I did. My father was nuts on the subject. He was bog Irish himself, so I guess he had to have someone to look down on. Anyway, it never happened.'

'No. The Japs came instead.'

'Right.' I occasionally had sentimental feelings about Australia and the Japanese threat but I didn't worry too much about it. I hadn't been back to the country since I skipped out in 1921 and I didn't have any impulse to visit. Still and all, I didn't want the Japanese to take it over. I guessed the Americans would have something to say about that.

'Well, the Japs and the Chinese have had a war. Still going on as far as I know. The Japs are winning but there's plenty of fight in the Chinese. Some of them are

Communists. I imagine they want to take the place over after we beat the Japs.'

'Most likely,' I said. 'Communists usually do like to run things, don't they? What's this got to do with us?'

'Damned if I know. I can tell you something about Hank, though. Name's Henry Hewson and he's got something to do with an organisation called "The Friends of Christian China". They've got a branch or a chapter in LA.'

I'd seen the police examine Hank's body and empty the pockets of his overall. I recalled a few keys, some money, spare bullets for the Winchester and that was about all.

Pete took his eyes off the road long enough to grin at me. 'I lifted a thing or two while you were out prowling in the woods. Might've handed them over if that Lieutenant and Sergeant had been nicer guys.'

I was full of admiration. 'You let them take your gun. You let them walk on you a bit. I should've known you had something up your sleeve.'

'Yup. You fit for some more work tonight?'

I wasn't, but how could I say it? The man had saved my life and provided us with a further lead to follow. He was a genius. Also, I was a bit drunk. I checked the .38 again, unnecessarily. 'Sure,' I said, 'where to?'

'Penseroso, 220A.'

Even in the 1940s, before the Puerto Ricans came in, Penseroso Street was a little too gamey for comfort. It was a mixed district, some coloured, some Mexicans, on the border with Chinatown. I figured that 220A would be at the Chinatown end of the street. That's how it turned out. Number 220A was a small stucco building from which the white paint was peeling. It looked like it could once have been a one-horse factory or storage depot; now it was a church going by the name of the 'Eastern Evangelical Mission'. The street itself was pretty respectable, with no more than two bars every block and no obvious vice. It was late on a Saturday night and the action was elsewhere. The church carried a sign saying that its first Sunday service would be at seven a.m.—Reverend Peter Moon presiding.

On one side the church was slap up against a three-storey apartment block; on the other there was a narrow cement walkway. We moved down it into the shadows and came up against a high gate. It was padlocked and I could hear a dog growling somewhere in the shadows. There were no lights on in the building.

'Guess we're going to church tomorrow, Rich?'

I nodded. I was dead tired but wanted to show willing. 'You didn't get anything else—home address, office?'

'Nope. I don't want to keep driving you around. Let's see if we can't find your Oldsmobile.'

It sounds ridiculous now, but it wasn't then. There weren't nearly as many cars on the road and not nearly the same turnover in stolen ones. Besides, Pete figured they had no use for my car so the driver would drop it off someplace where he could get transport. We drove around the downtown cab ranks and bus stations. We found the Olds near the Subway Terminal Building on South Street. The Red Cars ran out to the Valley,

Hollywood, Santa Monica, just about everywhere in those days. It was sitting by the kerb, undamaged with the windows wound up. I opened the door and felt for the keys. No dice. I swore. Hot-wiring cars has never been one of my favourite occupations.

'Check the floor,' Pete said.

I did and found the keys on the mat. There was also a crumpled cigarette packet down there with two butts in it. I gave one to Pete and lit us up.

'Thanks, Rich. Meet you at the church. Say, six forty-five. Don't be late.'

I grinned. Glad to have the heap back, glad to be smoking. 'What'll I wear?'

'Your gun,' Pete said and he waved and drove off.

I approached my apartment like a virgin coming into the bridal suite. I had the .38 at the ready in one hand and a tyre iron in the other. If I could've laid my hands on a blowpipe with poisoned darts I would have taken it along. I went through the front door and pasted myself against the wall. I sidled up the stairs in pretty much the same way, keeping my back firmly against the wall and looking up. I went up to the top level and checked all the possible hiding places before going to my door.

The lock on the door was slightly stronger than the kind you get on a cardboard suitcase. A cub scout could have opened it with his cap badge. I turned the key and snapped on the light but didn't go in. When nothing happened inside I put half my head around the door and saw why. It had already happened some time before—the place had been torn apart. The bed had been lowered and ripped open, the furniture had been pretty much smashed and the rug lifted and torn. My wooden filing cabinet was ready to serve as kindling and my files were torn and scattered around like ticker tape. Whoever it was had got mad looking for whatever it was. I didn't bother to clean up. I pushed the pieces of the bed together enough to form a support for the mattress and jammed the broken back of a chair up under the door knob. Then I took off my clothes and got into the bed. Immediately I felt the need for a piss so I had to get out, pull on a robe, open the door and use the john at the end of the passage.

I could hear people moving around in their apartments but it would be no use questioning them about my intruder. He or they must have made some noise, but so did most of my neighbours with their radios and phonographs. Swinging crowd in the Wilcox.

I went back to my room and noticed a card lying on the floor. I must have scuffed it clear of the debris. It was one of N. Robert Silkstein's cards and the scrawl on the back read: 'Call Mr Silkstein.' No please, no name. I put the chair back under the door and my gun down beside the bed. I put the card under the gun. I put my head on the half-wrecked pillow and went to sleep.

Ordinarily, after a day like the one I'd had, I wouldn't back myself to make a seven a.m. meeting, especially at a church. But I suppose I knew I wouldn't get a lot of sleep on the ruined Murphy bed and I was right. I tossed and turned, trying to avoid the sharp, broken end of a spring. I had dreams of Chinese coming in waves across frozen ground, throwing themselves at me with guns firing, not caring how many went down. (Korean vets later told me that this was pretty much the way it was over there ten years later. I'm very glad I didn't experience it for real.) The result was that I had a bath at about six a.m. and was shaved and, if not fresh, at least clean and full of coffee when I met Pete on Penseroso.

It was a cool, misty morning with some threat of rain in the air. I shivered a little in my lightweight suit. Pete was wearing a topcoat and a hat with a narrower brim. He looked less of a hayseed, more like a man who might go to church and think about what he heard. The street was almost deserted apart from a straggle of people, mostly Asians, standing around outside the church. They wore dark suits and hats and talked among themselves in tight little groups. The only other Anglos were an elderly couple who clung to each other as if for physical support and a couple of women, respectable-looking types in sensible hats.

Pete looked at his watch, said, 'Let's go,' and we joined the movement towards the front door.

As I hung my second-best hat on a peg in the small lobby I reflected that it must have been at least twenty years since I'd been in a church, maybe longer. About fifty people crowded into a space that could perhaps have accommodated a few more if the chairs had been pushed closer together. As it was, they were set in neat rows back from a raised platform where there was a lectern and a small table with a couple of chairs drawn up to it. A pile of battered hymn books sat on the chair at the end of each row and we passed them out among us.

The whole set-up was very bare and austere compared with the Anglican church and Sunday school I'd been compelled by my mother to attend in my childhood. I'd always associated religion with a lot of gold and red velvet and polished wood and stained glass, but I realised that was wrong. Despite the difference in the physical surroundings, this was the same ball game. It all had to do with the people—with the fear and false hopes that had been bred into them. Although most of the faces here were yellow with slanted eyes, they wore the same expressions as those back in Newcastle— desperately wanting to believe that the world was not as bad as it seemed.

I jerked my mind away from these unusually philosophical thoughts and studied the hymn book. It had been printed for the Chinese Mission Society in Shanghai in 1910 and was full of songs and prayers about converting the heathen. I glanced at Pete, who was carefully studying all the faces he could see. I did the same. A few more people had turned up, men and women. A few of the men were of the same stamp as Hank— thin, bitter-looking types. Suddenly, I urgently wanted a cigarette and a drink. Then there was a rustling among the congregation. Three people filed onto the platform —two women and a man. The man's head was lowered and turned away as he talked to the women, who sat down at the table and opened their hymn books. The man took his place behind the lectern. He was a big guy, wearing a dark suit, white shirt and tie. He lifted his head and faced us squarely. It was cold in the hall but that wasn't why I shivered. The man on the platform was Mr Brown, aka Charles Tan.

11

I felt Pete stiffen in the seat beside me, but then we were all up on our feet in response to a gesture from the man out in front.

'I see some strangers among us,' he said, looking not only at Pete and me but at a few other people in the room. 'You are welcome, friends. I am Reverend Moon and I have Mrs Armitage and Mrs Tan on the platform with me. Mrs Tan is going to say a few words on behalf of her committee a little later in the meeting. But first, a song and a prayer. 'Holy are the Heathen, too'— number nine.'

Someone up front produced a button accordion and the congregation launched into song. They all seemed to know the tune, what there was of it, and the words, as well. Most of them didn't even bother to open their books. I opened mine and Pete did the same and we mimed and faked our way through lines like, 'Though their skins may be yellow or black/Still their souls are as white as the snow'.

In the pause after the hymn, as we were sitting down, I hissed, 'It's him.'

'I dunno,' Pete said. 'Looks a bit different to me. Listen to the voice.'

I got plenty of opportunity to do that over the next twenty minutes. Moon spoke for all that time almost without drawing breath. He rattled on about the gallant struggle going on in China against the forces of darkness and how it was only sensible for the Christian world to want to make Christians of the country with more souls in it than any other.

'The world's churches have been sadly misguided,' he said. 'China should always have been the first priority. Imagine a flood of Chinese Christians pouring across the world. Imagine the good, the faith, the hope, the love...'

I could imagine a few other things coming from floods of Chinese, and I guessed the old guys running the religion racket in Rome, London and New York could do the same. But the message was getting through to the flock here on Penseroso. Heads were nodding and you could almost see the hands itching to go to the pockets and come out with the cash. I was pretty sure that this was a con. Well, all religion is, of course, but sometimes it's done with class. This was a crude appeal to a bunch of confused people who looked as if they might have a few bucks to spare.

Not that Moon wasn't a good speaker. He had a nice, rounded voice and he used it well, changing pace and pitch to keep the one point he had to make from becoming monotonous. That's the secret of preaching, as an old Tennessee faith healer once told me—'You got one thing to say. You goin' to burn in hell less'n you give me your money. You just gotta make it sound like somethin' more 'n that.' Well, Moon did and he had the crowd thirsty for more by the time he stopped and announced the next hymn.

'Well?' Pete whispered.

I'd been admiring the delivery so much I hadn't really thought about whether Moon was Tan or Brown. Now, as the accordion sounded the first notes, I wasn't sure either way. There'd been a roughness to Brown's voice, but also a certain theatricality. Moon was smooth, but he'd put an edge into things when he'd spoken about the 'barbaric sons of Nippon' with their 'worship of blood and steel'.

I shook my head. 'I don't know.'

'Shit,' Pete said. He drew a shocked look from the woman next to him, an elderly Chinese party dressed up like she was going to a funeral in Alaska. She had on a black wool dress that reached to the ground, black fur hat and a black fur piece wrapped around her neck.

I sneaked a quick look around the hall for any new faces, especially the kinds that go with lead-loaded saps and guns. But there was no-one like that. Just a lot of hopers and prayers, haters of sin and givers of money. We all stood up again and launched into 'Let us walk across the waters/ As Christ did long ago/ To hold out the hand of friendship/ To those who do not know.'

After that it was back on our bums again to listen to Mrs Armitage, who headed up the Committee for the Protection of Christian Orphanages in China, up again for 'A hundred million souls would make the Good Lord smile' and back down for the Reverend's wind-up. He had looked his captive audience over thoroughly and there had been no flicker of recognition in his eyes when he'd seen me. I stood a good couple of inches taller than any other man in the place, apart from Pete, so he couldn't have missed me. Mrs Tan hadn't said a thing. *Mrs Tan!* I pulled out a pen, scribbled the name on a page of the hymnal and showed it to Pete who nodded. This time, the dowager in the black fur shot me an evil look.

The Reverend spouted some more statistics and named a few people, Sun Yun this and Hung Yen that, who'd done great work in the field and then came his pitch.

'The collection box is at the door. Please give generously for the work. Also, add any suggestions you may have and the names of any you would wish a prayer to be said for. I will pray now for you all while you marshall your thoughts.'

And give you a chance to thumb through your wallets, I thought. Heads were hung all round and whispered voices uttered Chinese names and phrases. Then they were filing out and the sound was of shuffled feet, clinking coins and rustling banknotes. Mrs Tan and Peter Moon stood at the door talking to the faithful. There was much hand-pressing and whispering, much smiling and the brushing away of more than one tear. Pete and I sat where we were. When the body of the hall was empty there were just the four of us left— Pete and me, Moon and Mrs Tan.

'Can I help you, gentlemen?' He advanced towards us, big and bulky in his suit, expressing interest but absolutely no recognition. When he was close I could see slight differences—his skin was smoother than Brown/Tan's and his teeth were slightly less white. Otherwise, he was a dead ringer. I looked at Pete and shook my head. Pete produced one of his cards and handed it over.

97

Moon looked at it briefly. 'A private detective. I did not think that men of your stamp would be interested in our work.'

'We're interested in a man named Charles Tan, Mr Moon,' Pete said. 'He also goes by the name of Brown.'

There was a gasp from the end of the row. Mrs Tan had been standing there, maybe waiting for the signal to count the cash. Now she sank down into one of the seats and stared straight ahead of her.

Pete said, 'I guess that cuts out you saying you never heard of him, Reverend.'

Not liking to be left out of the scene too long, I got in with, 'And do you know a man named Henry Hewson?'

Moon inclined his head gravely. 'I think we had better have a talk, gentlemen. Mother, I have to talk to these men. Please excuse me for a few minutes.'

The old woman nodded.

'Hadn't you better secure the money?' I said.

Moon smiled. 'My mother lived through twenty-five years of war in China. She has a .22 pistol in her bag. The money is safe.'

He led us through to a small room at the back of the hall. There were four chairs around a table, a gas ring, a tap and a dresser. Moon took a teapot from the dresser and rinsed it out. He filled a saucepan with water and set it on the gas.

'Some China tea?'

'Sure,' Pete said. 'I had it in Frisco. It's good. I'll take a cup. I should introduce my colleague, Reverend— Mr Browning.'

'Tea, Mr Browning?'

'No thanks.' I took a seat wondering if it would be all right to smoke. But the room was part of the church. Probably not.

He made the tea, excused himself and took a cup out to pistol-packing Mrs Tan. When he got back he lowered himself into a chair, sipped at his tea and assumed a sad expression. 'It would seem you have had the misfortune to encounter my brother. I hope he did not harm you.'

I'd chewed and filed the broken thumbnail down to the quick. It didn't make much of a trophy now but I held it up just the same. 'He threatened to pull my fingernails out one by one. And he made a start.'

Moon shook his head. 'He is a violent and misguided man. How did you happen to fall foul of him?'

'I was hoping you could answer some questions for us, Reverend,' Pete said. 'Not the other way around.'

'Of course, of course. Well, Charles is my half-brother. He is several years older than me and his father was our mother's first husband. He was a bad man and my father, although his name also was Tan, was a good one. Moon, I might add, is a name I adopted for its symbolic value.'

It was the sort of explanation of character you get all the time. I go along with it pretty much, except that it doesn't explain the black sheep in a family, like me. Take my brother[14], he's... well, it doesn't matter. Moon went on to say that Mrs Tan brought her two children to the US in 1925 when Charles was twelve and Peter nine. She went back to China herself many

99

times over the next fifteen years rescuing war orphans from the cities and countryside. The boys were placed with relatives in San Francisco but still saw a lot of their mother.

'I worshipped her,' Moon said, 'and I still do. But perhaps the age difference was a problem, or the absence of a father... I do not know. But Charles turned out bad. He is a criminal.'

'Claimed he'd been in the marines,' Pete said.

Moon sipped his tea, which must have been cold by now. Pete had put his down long before. 'Briefly. Dishonourable discharge. Please, tell me what you are doing and I might be able to explain Charles's involvement.'

'We'd rather you told us where we can find him,' I said. 'We've got some cops asking questions about a dead man.'

Moon's eyebrows shot up. 'Really? Who?'

'Henry Hewson,' I said, 'known as Hank to your brother.'

Moon sighed. 'Henry was a troubled spirit. God rest his soul. Who killed him?'

'I did,' Pete said, 'before he could kill me. Come on, Reverend, what's going on? What's this all about?'

'All what?'

It was obvious then that we weren't going to get anything out of him without giving a little. Pete made a pretty good fist of the story and I have to admit that it sounded bizarre—abducted scriptwriter, missing niece of nightclub owner, kidnapped and tortured detective, ransacked apartment. Moon listened intently, dropping in the occasional question.

'You have spoken to this Singapore Sam? He had heard nothing about his niece?'

Pete and I exchanged looks. I shrugged. 'Sam's not the kind of man you go to and say, "I was with your niece and she got snatched." He's a dangerous man and he's got dangerous men working for him. We're assuming May Lin was involved somehow.'

'That is a comfortable assumption from your point of view.'

'There's nothing comfortable about this, Reverend,' Pete growled. 'Sallust's in a jam and we're in a jam with the Santa Monica cops. We could lose our licences. Now, I'll front Singapore Sam and his gorilla if I have to, but I prefer to understand things before I start throwing my weight around and I think you can help there.'

'Perhaps I can,' Moon said. 'More tea?'

We both declined but he made some more, probably to give him time to think. When he had the tea in front of him again, and my nerves were screaming for tobacco, he spoke for about twenty minutes. The gist of it was this—as well as the struggle against the Japanese there was a civil war brewing in China between the Nationalists and the Communists. He was full bottle on the subject and he made it fairly clear. Pete asked a question here and there that made it clearer. Moon said that there were certain treasures in China—art objects, manuscripts, relics that were being protected from the Japanese and sought after by both Nationalists and Communists. Apparently, to have possession of these things would confer legitimacy on any Chinese government.

Pete said, 'Who's got 'em now?'

'We cannot be sure, precisely. But the last information is that they were safe in the hands of monks and others sympathetic to the Nationalist cause.'

'Which side're you on?' I asked.

Moon spread his hands. 'That of the Kuomintang, the Nationalists. General Chiang is a good Christian. I should add that there is a third force, also interested. There are those who yearn for the restoration of the old imperial order in China, the Manchus. They, too, would wish to have possession.'

'Jesus,' Pete said. 'Excuse me, Reverend. But that's complicated.'

Moon said nothing. I was turning the information over in my mind, trying to remember what Brown/Tan and Hank had said. All I could recall was Hank babbling on about the Communists. Brown seemed to be supporting him, in a way. But it didn't figure. I said, 'I can't see your brother backing the Communists.'

'No,' Moon said. 'He would want the treasures for himself.'

12

There was a knock on the door and Mrs Tan came in. We all stood up the second she entered; she had that kind of presence. She was a small woman, dressed Chinese-style in a long dress with a high collar and mid-length brocaded jacket. Her hair was drawn back and she wore a black pillbox hat. She put a canvas bag on the floor and her large, black purse, the one with the gun in it no doubt, beside it. She took off her kid gloves, sat at the table and accepted a cup of tea.

'Your few minutes threatened to become an hour, son,' she said. 'I ran out of patience.'

'I'm sorry, mother. These gentlemen have been telling me a most disturbing story.'

Mrs Tan sipped tea and I got my first chance for a close look at her. Despite the get-up she wasn't a hundred per cent Chinese. There were many traces of the European in her features which she seemed to be trying to play down. That accounted for the less than fully Asian appearance of her sons. I wondered if the fathers were Eurasians too, and whether that counted for anything.

'I can guess,' Mrs Tan said. 'Charles is involved in some criminal activity which has touched our work here. That can only mean one thing—he is trying to secure the treasures.'

'That is what we suspect,' Moon said.

Mrs Tan snorted in an almost unladylike way. 'In order to sell them to the highest bidder. All he will do is ensure a knife between his ribs sooner rather than later. Tell me everything.'

Pete had got it off pat and honed down by this time and he ran through it quickly and smoothly without interruption from me or Moon. Mrs Tan sipped tea and permitted herself an occasional sniff.

'Very well,' she said when Pete stopped. 'Now you listen to me.'

She told us that she belonged to a family descended from the Chinese nobility and wealthy taipans. 'Both of my husbands were from this class,' she said. 'People of mixed blood exhibit many varieties of character. With Peter and myself, there is a burning wish to give to China the best of European civilisation, that is, the Christian religion.'

Moon nodded. 'And to make amends for the wrongs done to the Chinese people by European plunderers and politicians.'

'Just so,' Mrs Tan said. 'Unhappily, some of our kind display the worst characteristics of both races. Charles, I regret to say, is one of these. He cares nothing for God or man in any form, Chinese, European or anything in between.'

'That's a hard thing to say about your own boy,' Pete murmured.

'It is. But the truth must be told.' Mrs Tan sighed. 'In some ways, this present trouble is the fault of Peter and myself. Charles must have heard us talking about the Imperial treasures and the plans being made...'

'What plans?' Pete said.

Mrs Tan glanced at her son. He inclined his head and she went on. 'It has been suggested that certain of these... items should come to America, for safekeeping.'

That gave Pete and me reason to exchange nods. This was something I could understand at last—loot.

'Perhaps the most important of the treasures is a piece of jade. Do you gentlemen know anything about jade?'

Pete and I said 'No' together.

'Fei Tsui jade is a rare and wonderful material. Because of its rarity it is valuable in itself, not just because of the workmanship that might have gone into carving it. But the Emblem of the Sun and Moon and Stars has incalculable value in every respect. Let me explain. It is a large piece of Fei Tsui jade in the form of a perfect half sphere. It is inlaid with a sizeable piece of gold, which represents the sun, and several perfect pearls which represent the moon and stars. The moon pearl is very large and very valuable.'

'Sounds to me as if this dingus could be broken down into a lot of valuable merchandise,' Pete said.

Mrs Tan shuddered slightly. 'Indeed. But that must never be allowed to happen. You are looking somewhat sceptical, Mr Browning.'

I turned my hat around in my hands. 'I don't know,' I said. 'Maybe I just need a smoke and my brains are drying out. But just from your description, Mrs Tan, the thing sounds pretty, well, vulgar. I don't quite see...'

Mrs Tan would have flipped her fan if she'd had one. 'You are exactly right! It *is* vulgar, extremely so, which is why the peasants and other ignorant people value it so highly and why anyone wishing to hold power in China aspires to possess it.'

'Like the Crown Jewels, I suppose,' I said. 'Though I don't imagine that if I got hold of them I could set myself up as Richard the...'

'Fourth,' Mrs Tan smiled. 'No, but China is in many ways a very primitive country. Such insignia matter very much to the common people, as they did back in the days of Richard the Third.'

On British history she left me standing as, I suspected, she would on most subjects. She was a very sharp old lady.

Like me, Pete was impressed, but he hadn't been sapped and kidnapped the day before and possibly hadn't been drunk recently. He weighed in with the key question.

'What's this got to do with Hart Sallust? I can't see him wanting to get hold of the dingus for himself, or for the Nationalists or Communists, for that matter.'

'No,' Mrs Tan said. 'But his wife would.'

I shook my head. 'He hasn't got a wife. No woman would stay with him long enough to take out a licence.'

'True, the man is a drunkard, a brawler and a womaniser,' Mrs Tan said. 'Nevertheless, he has a wife. Her name is Sue Feng and she is an agent of the Kuomintang.'

'It's hard goods to buy,' Pete said. We were out on the street, leaning against my car and smoking, at last.

With what I thought was commendable generosity, until I remembered it would go on Bobby Silkstein's bill, Pete had contributed twenty bucks to the Reverend Moon's fighting fund. It was a polite way to pay for what could turn out to be a crucial piece of information. Mrs Tan had given us the address of a man who *might* be able to lead us to Sue Feng. She asked only that if we were ever in a position of power in respect to Charles Tan, we should temper justice with mercy. There was no problem with that to non-vindictive types like Pete and myself. The only problem was, the address was in San Francisco. We were mulling this over as we smoked and felt the sun finally begin to dispel the morning's dampness.

'Could be a trick to get me out of town,' Pete said.

'That'd mean you think Moon and Mrs Tan aren't straight.' I flicked ash onto the road. 'And I'd trust them further than I'd trust my own mother.'

Pete sighed. 'I guess so. I still can't add it all up. What d'you make of it?'

I shook my head. 'You'd do better to ask Chandler.'

'That's not a bad idea. Listen, Rich, I want you to stay with me on this case.'

'Do I see some money?'

'Sure.' He fished out his wallet and peeled off a couple of twenties.

'I lost a good hat,' I said.

He gave me another twenty and then told me what he wanted done. My first thought was to give him the money back, but that's a hard thing to do, especially when you haven't got any coming in to take its place.

I didn't mind going to talk about things with Raymond Chandler, that was the easy part. The hard part was going down to Santa Monica and telling Lieutenant Burt Martingdale and Sergeant Hamer that Mr McVey couldn't keep the appointment because he'd gone to San Francisco.

I went west on Whittier, stopping for lunch at a truckers' cafe this side of Century City. I had nothing in particular to say to Martingdale and planned to play dumb if he tried to get me to tell him what McVey was up to. As it turned out, I didn't have to worry. At Santa Monica police headquarters everything was quiet, it being Sunday, but there was a fat, old desk sergeant nodding behind a pile of paper and an ashtray which it seemed to be his main job to keep filled. He woke up long enough to tell me that Martingdale and Hamer were working on a murder.

'Juicy one at Marina del Rey,' the sergeant said. 'Actress and a priest. Gun and pills. The lieutenant's out there trying to get his picture in the papers so's he can make captain quicker.'

'What about Hamer?'

The sergeant snorted. 'Same thing, so's he can make lieutenant.'

'I thought you had to take a test for that?'

'You do. Me, I failed three times, but Hamer passed it last year. Now, he needs a little juice.'

I thought I knew what he meant. There were probably more qualified sergeants around than lieutenant's jobs. If

Hamer could get an edge, like involvement in a cover-up or the suppression of evidence, he could go to the head of the queue. I gave the sergeant my card and asked him to make a note of the time. Then I got out of there as fast as I could, in case I ran into the lieutenant by chance. With any luck, his priest–actress job would keep him so busy he'd forget about his two private eyes. At least it would buy us some time.

I got back into my car in a lot better frame of mind. I even considered driving north to look for my lost hat. But a flash of Charles Tan with his pliers and a memory of the cold, clear air around that cabin in the mountains, cured me of that idea. Smog is safer. I'd never much liked wearing hats anyway; losing one was no big deal and there was no-one happier than me when the damn things went out of fashion in the 1960s. 'Course that's easy for me to say that's always had a full head of hair. I knew bald guys that hung on to their hats into the seventies, praying that they'd come back into style. Luck of the draw. I strolled around Santa Monica for a while, just to tell myself I wasn't spooked. I didn't like what I saw. I had a few drinks in a bar that made me like it a little bit better but not much. There seemed to be something heartless about the place, as if it was filled with people who were on the make and would leave the minute they made their score. I bought cigarettes and headed back to Los Angeles where people stayed, even after they made their score.

The woman who came to the door of the house on Drexel looked to be about seventy-five, but she made up and dressed as if she was less than half that age. Her hair was a pink cloud and she was wearing something soft and white and billowing that would have been a knockout on Gene Tierney, but not on her. Her mouth was a puckered, scarlet hole and the false eyelashes she wore had picked up a lot of white dust from the make-up plastered on her face.

'Yes, young man?'

'Er, good afternoon, Mrs Chandler. My name is Richard Browning. I wonder if Raymond is in?'

The plucked eyebrows shot up like flushed birds. 'Do you have a card?'

Very formal, for Hollywood. I fished out a card and gave it to her. She wore gold-rimmed reading glasses on a long gold chain. She lifted them and placed them on her well-shaped nose. In fact, everything about her was well-shaped, it was just that she was trying to pretend that half a century hadn't passed. She read the card and handed it back; that's what happens when you're not important. Mostly you can re-use the card, but not this time. She must have been eating something sweet because the card felt sticky when I took it back.

'My husband isn't at home,' she said. 'He's at a party. I was not well enough to attend.'

Husband! I'd figured her for Chandler's mother and had started to form a few questions in my mind about that. If this old dame was his wife, there'd have to be new questions. I tried to conceal my surprise and asked, 'Would you mind telling me where the party is? It's rather urgent that I see Mr Chandler.'

'Is it about a *crime*? Raymio would be so thrilled!'
'Yes, it is.'
'Well, the party's at Buddy Smiles's place in Beverly Hills. Where else? Summit Drive, I believe. Raymio thinks he's going to get a job by going to this affair, but I doubt it. More likely, he'll get a hangover.'

I jotted down the address on the back of my card, avoiding the sticky parts where the ink wouldn't sit. I tipped my hat and thanked her.

'Just a minute, young man.' A hand, skin wrinkled like an old lizard and with almost every finger carrying a ring, reached out and clutched at my wrist. I looked down into blue eyes that time had washed almost white and at a face that was a mask of disappointment.

'Yes, ma'am?'
'When you see him, please tell him not to be late. I'm not feeling well. I need him.'
'Okay.'
'And tell him to be careful driving. That Buick's too big for him. He's not a big man, like you.'
'No, ma'am. I'll...'
'But he's a wonderful man, my Raymio. He's a wonderful man, Mr Browning. And a great writer, even though he thinks I don't know it.'

I said, 'Yes, ma'am,' and fled.

13

Buddy Smiles was unique. God only knows what his real name was and where he came from, but he'd been a highly successful comedian, teaming up with people like Harry Langdon and Harold Lloyd. Comedy must be a pretty hard business because most of the big-time comics ended up drunks or crazy. Not Buddy Smiles; he'd invested in Beverly Hills real estate rather than stocks and bonds and so he survived the crash in '29. When his kind of joking ran out of steam ten years later and he got too fat to be funny, he went into producing. Now he was one of the powers in the land— the Napoleon of Beverly Hills, Hedda had called him. Or was it the Wellington? Doesn't matter, Buddy Smiles had the yea or nay on picture projects, and there's no greater power than that in Hollywood.

Up Summit Drive past Pickfair which, after Doug and Mary broke up, was just somewhere for her to get on with her drinking. I used to have a modest place there myself back in the old days[15] when you could gas up your car and get drunk, all for five dollars. Smiles's place was a six-acre lot with everything crammed onto it that a man needs to be comfortable and a good few he doesn't really need—pool, tennis court, skeet range, par three hole, gym, steam room. Word was that Smiles invited young men and women out there to play games and have fun and he joined in as the spirit moved him.

It didn't sound like the sort of place for Raymond Chandler, but you never can tell. After all, a guy who marries a woman twenty years older than himself has got to have some kinks.

There was a party going on all right. The cars were parked along the road for a hundred yards on either side of the gate and there must have been at least as many again inside the property. I knew there was no point in trying to go through the gate. These affairs were invitation only and the sorts of guys who asked for your invitation were cousins of the types who'd rattled my brain-box the day before. Fortunately, as a former resident, I knew the lie of the land. The big shots' houses were all high-security glamour at the front and for a short distance along the perimeter, but the interest and the money started to run out a bit further back. I was pretty sure that 'The Summit', Smiles's place, would be the usual dry gulch a hundred yards past the house and pool, where the irrigation stopped and the mesquite and mariposa began.

I parked my car and got out. I smoked a cigarette and looked the spread over. Then I took off my jacket and folded it so I could carry it. This exposed the .38 in the hip holster. *What the hell?* I thought. *Give the natives a thrill.* I loosened my tie and walked up the road to the fence that divided Smiles's property from the next one, which wasn't nearly so well-maintained. I entered the next-door place and worked my way back through the overgrown garden, keeping clear of the house. The clouds had cleared, allowing the sun to turn on some late afternoon heat.

I was sweating by the time I'd got past Smiles's neighbour's house. I had to work my way to the fence through scruffy garden beds to orient myself. I was almost past Smiles's various entertainment areas, but I could still hear sounds of jollity. I pushed on, trying to avoid picking up leaves and spider webs and to keep out of the way of thorns and prickles and all the other things that make the great outdoors hell to the civilised man. Eventually I was in the badlands, the dry country beyond the taps and sprays where the run-off water cuts the hillsides into lamingtons[16]. The back of this place was a wasteland; the back of 'The Summit' was a garbage dump.

There was no dividing fence. I picked my way through the scrub until I was standing a couple of hundred yards directly behind Buddy Smiles's house. He probably didn't know that his yardman dumped the bottles and other trash down here when he forgot to put it out for collection. I'd say this was one time in ten—there were an awful lot of bottles. Some of the garden refuse had been dumped here too—lopped branches, grass clippings and weeds. There was an old tennis net, decayed garden furniture and other such items.

I skirted around the rubbish and moved forward to where the lawn began, which still put me a long way short of the house. I was hot and thirsty and the thirst made me bold. I pulled on my jacket and tramped up through the garden and past the tennis court until I reached poolside. The pool was half enclosed by a glass wall and half roofed with some transparent material. There were several people standing around talking and drinking, a couple of men and women in the water, and a guy doing fancy dives off a low board. There was also a trestle table with food and drinks set out on it. I marched up, grabbed a bottle of beer from a cooler and poured it into a mug. I put it down in about three gulps and poured another. I spread some stuff on a chunk of bread and wolfed it down so fast I didn't even taste it.

I was starting on the second beer and contemplating the meat platter when a strong hand gripped me below the elbow.

'Might I see your invitation, sir?'

The guy wore a monkey suit but he was no monkey. He was about twenty-five and in his prime. I'd have had as much chance against him as against Joe Louis. Still, I knew enough to just lift my arm so that if he wanted to keep holding it he'd end up looking pretty silly. He let go and I took out a card.

'Browning,' I said. 'Security. I came up the back way. I could've marched a platoon up there and taken over the swimming pool.'

He was young and blond and strong and not very bright. He looked at the card and blinked. There wasn't a lot on it to read, but he seemed to be having trouble.

'I think you better come and talk to Mr Campesi. He's handling security.'

Just then the diver left the board, went well up and into a nice pike and hit the water cleanly. Some of the people standing around gave him a modest hand and my friend was distracted. One thing at a time would always be his motto. The diver swam to the side of the pool and climbed out. This put him only a few feet away. He flicked hair and water from his eyes and stared at me. I stared back.

'Mr Browning,' he said. 'How do you do.'

I can recover fast when I have to. 'Nice dive, Mr Chandler,' I said.

He pulled himself out of the pool and nodded when an attendant handed him a robe. The blond guy who'd grabbed me had backed away a little and he retreated still further when Chandler told him that everything was all right. He took his pipe out of the pocket of the robe as he spoke and this seemed to be the convincer.

Monkey Suit said, 'Yes sir,' and went off to look for someone else to annoy.

Chandler got his pipe lit and gestured at a table near the pool. I grabbed my beer and joined him. He puffed smoke into the warm air and took a pull on a highball that was medium dark. I guess I was gaping just a little.

'Show I turn on for the peasants,' Chandler said. 'The trouble with California is that nobody has ever been taught to do anything properly. Take these people. They all ride and swim and play tennis, but not properly. Same with writing. Lots of people in this town can write but not one in a hundred knows how a sentence works. Where did you go to school, Mr Browning?'

'Er, Dudleigh. Little private school in Australia.'

'What the English call a public school. Good. I bet you know what a noun clause is.'

I tried to look as if I might, although I hadn't the faintest idea. This was a different Chandler from the house mouse of Drexel Avenue. He was carrying a bit of weight but his body looked solid, and the wet hair hanging across his forehead gave him a raffish air. He reminded me somewhat more of the Canadian army sergeant in the shellhole twenty-five years ago.

'Have you seen Buddy Smiles? Got a deal going?'

Chandler waved his pipe. 'Seen him and dismissed the man. A philistine. No, no deal.'

I realised then that he was just a bit drunk, which was probably how he got up the nerve to put on a diving exhibition for Smiles's guests. No-one seemed to mind that the show was over; they cruised around in ones and twos, the young and beautiful and the not so young and ugly. I could hear music coming from the house. A man pushed a girl into the pool. Nobody laughed, so that evidently wasn't going to catch on. People started to drift away from the pool. There didn't seem to be anybody wanting to catch Chandler's eye or ear. It was as good a time and place as any for a talk.

I told Chandler what Pete and I had done and learned since we'd last seen him. This took me through another two beers and put him well down in another highball. Being an experienced and responsible drinker, I kept eating as I was drinking and I tried to get Chandler to do the same. He refused. It looked like he was one of those who gave up eating when he drank.

'Pete said you might have some ideas.'

Chandler pulled the robe closer around him. I hadn't noticed that the light had dropped as I'd been talking and that it was getting cool. 'The San Francisco angle is good,' he murmured. 'Yes, I like the San Francisco angle. 'Course, that's Hammett's territory.'

'Who?'

'Dashiel Hammett.'

'Who's he? I never heard of him. Is he a cop?'

'No.' Chandler was staring past me at a redhead who was dipping her toe in the pool. She wore a brief one-piece swimsuit and her body was very white and firm. Chandler's eyes devoured her. The redhead shook her head, flicked the water from her foot and sashayed away.

'Is this Hammett somebody Pete should see in Frisco? Does he have connections in Chinatown or something?'

Chandler shivered. Suddenly he looked owl-like and older than his years again. 'I wouldn't be a bit surprised, but no, Hammett's not a cop. He was a detective once, or so he claims. I've always doubted it myself. Hammett's a writer. A damned good one.'

'A writer. What...?'

Chandler finished his drink and seemed to fight a battle with himself over whether to have another or not. No decision. He leaned forward and jabbed his pipe stem at me; if either of us had been a bit drunker he might have put my eye out.

'I told you that the whole key to this thing lies in what Sallust's writing.'

'We tried to find out, but we couldn't.'

'Didn't try hard enough. Listen, has Sallust got a bolt-hole anywhere, some place he'd go if he got in a jam?'

I thought about it while Chandler made himself another drink. 'He's got a sister here,' I said. 'He brought her out from the east but she hated the movie business. I think she works in a library.'

'Perfect,' Chandler growled. 'And you say he's a booze hound, like all of us?'

'Right.'

'Ever go on the wagon?'

'Me? No, not unless...'

'Not you, Sallust.'

'Oh, sure, lots of times.'

'Okay. You find where his sister lives and you go there and find the place where he hides his booze when he's supposed to be on the wagon. I know all about it. There'll be a place. Under the bath, in a typewriter case, in a pigeon loft. There's a place.'

'Suppose I do that. Then what?'

'If he's writing anything different, or dangerous, or even good, he'll keep a copy hidden somewhere. His booze hole's the most likely spot.'

It seemed like a long shot and I was suspicious of Chandler's tendency to mix up writing with real life. I couldn't tell whether his judgments on people were drawn from fiction or reality. Maybe it didn't matter. It was a lead, anyway, something to do while McVey was in San Francisco. I thanked him and got up to leave.

'Just a minute, Browning. How did you know I was here?'

'Your wife told me.'

'Oh.'

That was the moment to deliver her message, to tell him to hurry home because she wasn't well. Somehow, I just couldn't do it. With his hair ruffled and the pipe jutting from his jaw, he didn't look too bad. His body, wrapped in the robe, looked hard and compact and his legs were okay. He was a little on the short side, but if Alan Ladd was around somewhere he could stand next to him and look tall. Maybe he'd get lucky with one of the spare women wandering around the place. I hoped so. I shook his hand and told him I'd keep him informed on our progress with the case.

'Please do. It's an intriguing matter. Did you learn Latin at Dudleigh, Browning?'

'Yes, but I...'

'Never mind. I'd only be showing off. I do that too much. Tell Pete McVey to be sure to come and see me. I need to talk to him some more about that plate in his head. That interests me [17].'

I said 'Sure' and moved away from the pool where the water had grown dark as the light of the day died. The blond bouncer picked me up again as I made to walk through the house.

'You're leaving, sir?'

'Yeah, I thought I might just say goodbye to the host.' In fact I'd spotted Joan Crawford, in a shimmering black dress, through the glass doors. I've always had a thing for Joan Crawford and I wanted to get a good look at those shoulders and that mouth, close up.

'I think not, sir,' the bouncer said. 'If you'd just come with me this way, I'll escort you to the gate. Needless to say, Mr Campesi has never heard of you. I'm authorised to treat gatecrashers firmly.'

'I bet you enjoy it, too.' I let him manoeuvre me towards a side path. What the hell? The shoulders were probably padded and the mouth couldn't possibly be as sexy as it looked on the big screen. I realised that

I was randy. It had been some time. Maybe I could could call a few numbers and *I* could get lucky. We went down a bricked walkway under a pergola covered with some sweet-smelling vine. Nice to be rich. Nice to drink champagne and invite Joan Crawford to your parties and...

Something glinted in the glow cast by the outdoor party lights. I saw that the bouncer was slipping on a pair of brass knucks. I reached behind me for the .38— an overreaction and way too slow anyway. Then a voice cut through the sweet-scented air.

'Dick! What're you doing here? Just the man I wanted to see.'

It was N. Robert Silkstein, my agent. Resplendent in a white suit with a long panatella between his fingers and a sinewy blonde on his arm, he reached enthusiastically for my hand.

I switched from going for my gun to shaking hands, always a wise choice. 'Hello Bobby,' I said. 'It's good to see you.'

Silkstein pointed his cigar at the bouncer, who was hiding the knucks in his jacket pocket. 'What's this guy doing?'

I smiled at the blonde, who wore a vague, drunken or doped look, and moved closer to Silkstein.

'It's all right, Bobby. He mistook me for Errol Flynn. Flynn fucked his mother and his sister and his wife and he wanted a little talk.'

The bouncer brought his hand up, minus the brass knuckles, but in a pretty convincing fist. He stopped the punch a half inch short of my nose. 'I'm taking a stroll for ten minutes, peeper,' he growled. 'When I come back, be missing.'

14

Bobby Silk was a little guy, starting to fill out now as he entered his forties. He'd also started to step out, it seemed. The thin blonde certainly wasn't his wife and they hadn't gone out into the shrubbery to talk horticulture. The blonde still seemed to be keen to get on with what they had intended to do, and she became pouty when Bobby made it clear it was business first. That was Bobby.

'Go inside and get us a drink, babe,' he said. 'Mine's a scotch on the rocks. What about you, Dick?'

'The same.'

'Take your time, sugar,' Bobby said, 'and don't worry. You and your career are at the top of my list.'

The blonde pouted some more and walked away, letting us see the sway of her lean hips and the movement of her firm little arse. Bobby watched her out of sight. Bobby's father had been one of the great Hollywood lechers, insatiable for women morning, noon and night. Eventually it had killed him. Bobby, despite his opportunities, had always resisted temptation, but it looked as if he was running true to his breeding now.

'The next Betty Grable,' he said.

'Too thin.'

'Damn sight easier to put a few pounds on 'em than to take it off.' He steered me in the direction of a seat under a palm tree. We sat down. I lit a cigarette and

Bobby lit his cigar. Something else new—I'd never known him to smoke before. His father went through a box a day. 'Now, Dick, where've you been keeping yourself? I've been calling. I even sent someone round with a note for you.'

I'd been so caught up in the Sallust case that I'd forgotten the card from Bobby. Also, I hadn't appreciated the favour that had been bestowed on me. Hollywood agents expected people to contact *them*, not the other way around.

'I've been busy, Bobby.'

'Doing what? You're not working.'

His little eyes went narrow and shrewd. Even Bobby, who made a six-figure income, would scream if he heard that a small-time actor like me was in work and not forking over the commission. I considered what to tell him and decided that it might as well be the truth. He was the principal, after all. He'd hired Pete McVey and McVey had hired me. No harm in the 2IC turning in an interim report. I gave him a brief version of what Pete and I had done, glossing it a little, making us look on the ball.

Bobby listened with growing impatience. I was surprised. I thought I was telling it pretty good. When I finished talking he waved it all away with the hand that held the cigar. 'Forget all that.'

'Eh?' I said. I felt as if the ground had opened under me. I wished the next Betty Grable would come back with the drinks.

'They've lowered the boom on that project,' Bobby said. 'Garfield's got a deferment and the producer, Joe

Herman, he's out. So that drunken bum can't turn in his script. Who cares? He's all washed up. If McVey runs up a big tab in Frisco he could end up holding it. I'm terminating him, as of now.'

I have to admit I was shocked. Even for Hollywood, even for Bobby Silk, this was pretty barefaced. I was trying to think of something to say when the girl came back with the drinks. She was wearing a clinging white cocktail dress, short in the skirt and low in front. She'd discarded the light wrap she'd had around her shoulders and I revised my opinion—maybe thin wasn't exactly the word. Bobby introduced her as Suzie something or other. She never did become the next Betty Grable but she did become Bobby's second wife and got off with a good chunk of loot in the end, so I guess she has no kicks coming.

Bobby was certainly very attentive that night. He gave her his jacket when she shivered and lit her cigarettes while we chatted about her acting career. She'd had a bit part in *Stage Door Canteen* and was hoping for a few lines in *Meet Me in St Louis*. Bobby was all encouragement. When he'd fed her ego enough, he turned to me and flicked his cigar away into the bushes where it died in a shower of sparks.

'Dick,' he said, 'how'd you like to go out to Australia?'

I was so taken aback I didn't know what to say. Like all Australians who travel, I knew that there was no other country on earth like it. No place with the same smells and combination of sun and earth and sea. Not many are able to leave the place and never go back, no matter how much they hate the wowsers and the bootlickers and the politicians like that little rat, Billy Hughes. With me, it depended on my mood of the moment. Sometimes, I could see a photograph of a kangaroo and feel something throb inside me that I guess you could call homesickness. Other times, I'd remember the churches in Melbourne, Long Bay Gaol in Sydney or, even worse, my first wife, Elizabeth McKnight, and I'd look around me and thank god I was in California. That night, at Buddy Smiles's preposterous house on Summit Drive, I was caught between the two reactions.

'Er, I don't know, Bobby,' I said. 'What's on your mind?'

Bobby tapped his nose. 'A picture. What else?' Suzie snuggled closer to him and giggled.

I said 'What picture? I told you, I'm not working with Flynn again.'

'I know, I know. Nothing to do with Errol, this one. It's a war picture. Set in the South Pacific. I reckon I can get you the part of the Australian general who's kicking Japanese ass in New Guinea.'

'*Are* we kicking ass in New Guinea? I thought...'

Bobby had another cigar going. He waved it and Suzie giggled again. 'That's a detail. Point is, it's a propaganda movie. Morale-boosting stuff. And if you do it, you'd have to go out to Australia and liaise with the Army there. Whaddya say, Dick? You're in line for it. Take my word.'

When an agent says 'Take my word' you know it's time to start sniffing for lies. But Bobby had sought me out and seemed sincere, sincere enough to put the blonde on the back burner for a while and still be eyeballing me like he meant it. I even had the feeling that I could've touched him for a loan, and *that* kind of a feeling has to be attended to.

'Tell me more about the picture,' I said.

Bobby reached up to put his arm around my shoulder. It was a very uncomfortable position for both of us and I realised that he only did it so he could whisper in my ear. 'War picture, like I said. Titled *South Pacific Showdown* at the moment. That could switch. Location stuff in Bris-bane and New Guinea. Looking at Spencer for the US general who goes *mano a mano* with your character. Dramatic stuff. Bette Davis for Spence, Marilyn Maxwell for you unless casting can come up with some Australian twist, maybe British.'

Suzie squealed again. 'Bobby! Whisperin's rude!'

'Sorry, baby. Hush hush. Great chance, Dick. I sold them on your flying for Hughes and your Canadian army papers.'

This is the dilemma the less-than-heroic always face. I had a brave man's credentials, won mostly by cunning, and I was constantly being forced to live up to them. Tricky, but after twenty-five years I was getting used to it. 'So, what do I have to do?'

'That's my boy,' Bobby chortled. 'Be at Paramount tomorrow morning at eightsky, super-sharp.'

'What for?'

'Screen test. What else?'

'I thought you said I could have it.'

Bobby had me hooked and he knew it. That meant he had the upper hand and there was nothing he liked better than showing it. 'I told them that if they wanted an Aussie who knew that New Guinea wasn't in Africa and who could wear a general's suit, you were the man. Show up sober and you'll get it. Wouldn't hurt to brush up on a few of them salty down-under expressions.'

'Stone the crows,' I said. 'Fair dinkum.'

Bobby waved his cigar. 'Yeah, that sorta thing.'

We'd finished our drinks by this time and there didn't seem to be anything more to say. On one level, the idea of going to Australia as a make-believe army officer scared me stiff. After all, I'd deserted from the Australian army. But that was a long time ago and I'd been going under the name of Hughes at the time. I doubted that many people still alive in Australia would even recognise me. And it's one thing to sneak back into a country on your uppers and looking for a handout (as I'd come close to doing a few times in my hand-to-mouth existence) and arriving in triumph as a Paramount leading man playing opposite Spencer Tracy.

I imagined the arrival scene: Dick Browning perhaps, get away from the old Richard. A new image. A bit grey at the temples but obviously only in his early forties. Way too young to be Richard Kelly Browning of Newcastle and other parts. The studios had experts at washing dirty stories from the past so that they came up shiny bright in the present.

There was more to it than that, though. I'd been in Hollywood on and off for more than twenty years and I'd never landed a solid, leading role. I'd been close, but something always seemed to happen—I'd be forced to appear under an assumed name or my scenes would be left in the cutting room. I'd never made it and I'd seen some awful types who had—I'm thinking primarily of Flynn, of course. Maybe it wasn't too late. Maybe I could carve out a career as the distinguished older man, mostly the life-scarred veteran, but occasionally getting the younger woman and holding her against the young Turks. I could see it and I liked it.

I winked at Bobby—the conspirator, the give-it-a-go-boy. 'I'll be there.'

'Great. Now, Suzie and me'd better get back in there 'n' mingle.'

A squeal of protest. 'Bobby!'

Bobby put his arms around her and gave her a squeeze. He was all-agent now, all-studio, all-American. 'Think of your career, honey-pie. There's important people inside.'

'You're important people to me, Bobbykins.'

'Yeah, well... okay, the night is young. Ah, you should get some beauty sleep, Dick. They want a battered military man, sure, but you look like you've fought a hundred Japs single-handed. You need a doctor eelgood to set you up for tomorrow? I know a guy out in Glendale...'

I moved away, half-randy, half-sober. 'I'll be fine, Bobby. Just tell me one thing. What would you have done if you hadn't seen me tonight? Who would you have thrown this job to?'

'Victor McLaglen[18]. Over the hill but...'

'He's not even an Australian! He was born in England.'

Bobby shrugged. 'Any port in a storm, Dick. I'll be hoping to hear from Paramount, tensky.'

15

Everyone knows the Paramount gate on Marathon. Getting past it if you didn't have the right ticket was harder than getting to see the Pope. When I showed up on Monday morning, showered, shaved and wearing the best clothes I could salvage from my ransacked room at the Wilcox, I gave my name to the gateman and waited. It was already warm and the jacket I was wearing was a shade too heavy. I was sweating and the guy took his time. *What if it was all a practical joke of Bobby's?* I thought. *What if he had a camera there waiting to snap me as I sweated and waited?* That's Hollywood for you. A perpetual itch between the shoulder-blades.

The gateman touched his cap. 'You can go in, Mr Browning. Here's your pass. Sound stage four, on your right.'

I went in under the wrought-iron gate to Paradise, clutching my pass and still sweating. Along the asphalt, between the flower beds to sound stage four. Another guard, but the pass was an open sesame. I went out of the sunlight into a big, dim barn where the temperature was about twenty degrees lower than outside. The concrete floor was criss-crossed with wires and cables. When they turned the lights on, the temperature would zoom up thirty degrees. It was no wonder the movie people were always getting colds and shooting themselves full of drugs to cope. I knew that, and that there'd be some little Hitler of a director telling me how to wipe my nose. And I still wanted it.

A young woman carrying a clipboard hurried towards me. I gave her my name; she checked it on her list and handed me another pass. The first one was was red, this was white; I wondered when I'd get the blue one.

'I'm Patty King. Mr Herman and Mr Farrow are in studio two, Mr Browning. They'd like you to join them. If you'd just follow me.'

'What about Mr Tracy and Miss Davis?' I said.

She put her finger to her lips. 'Shh. Walls have ears.'

The shoulder-blade itch again. This was weird. I remembered Bobby Silk's uncharacteristic effort to get in touch with me and his whispering about the cast list. Something funny was going on. I stepped over the cables, following Patty King's shapely form, and tried to figure out what it might be. Joe Herman was an independent producer and the guy supposed to be involved in the mysterious picture Hart Sallust was working on. But this couldn't have anything to do with *that*! We were inside Paramount Pictures—studio numero uno, as the gossip mags called it. Tracy and Davis weren't Paramount players, I knew that. Maybe the secrecy was all about some inter-studio deal. Maybe.

I squared my shoulders and tightened my jawline and marched into the room Patty King indicated. I recognised Farrow—a strongly-built, athletic-looking guy with piercing blue eyes and an intelligent expression. The other man, Herman presumably, was the opposite—he was enormously fat, fat all over—

golf-ball-sized pouches under his eyes, three chins and another on the way.

Patty King made the introductions and I shook Farrow's hard, dry hand and Herman's moist, soft one. The room was some kind of technician's work space, with lots of sound and recording equipment lying around. We sat in straight-back chairs drawn up to an old white pine table that had about a thousand telephone numbers scratched on it. Strange place for a meeting. Miss King brought coffee; Herman lit a cigar and I had my first Lucky of the day. Farrow rolled himself a cigarette with tobacco from a pouch. He took a long time over it, getting the tobacco to sit evenly, tucking in the loose strands.

'You have seen military service I understand, Mr Browning?' Herman said.

Tricky territory. Best to play it confident. I puffed smoke and nodded. 'Right. The first war, closing stages. I was just a kid. I fought in the Mexican revolution for a while. Bloody shambles. I was in the Canadian army for a time, too.'

Farrow drank some coffee and kept playing with his cigarette. It was just about perfect by this time but he still wasn't happy. His voice was pretty much American with just a trace of British in it. I couldn't hear any Australian but then, I don't guess there was much of the old bowyang and bunyip[19] in mine, either. 'That's quite impressive. I understand you fly planes as well?'

Never again if I can help it, I thought. 'I did, for a time. Pretty rusty now, of course.'

'We have got all the crazy fliers we want,' Herman said. 'We need authenticity, integrity, dignity...'

I tried to exhibit all those qualities in good measure, as I smoked my cigarette and drank my coffee.

Farrow had got as far with his cigarette as wetting the end so it wouldn't stick to his lips. I wondered if he was ever going to smoke it. 'How much did your agent tell you about this project?' he said.

I'd picked up the drift by now—early morning meeting, no-one around but the super-efficient and discreet Miss King, multiple passes... 'Very little,' I said. 'I got the impression that it's not something for Hedda and Louella just yet.'

Farrow snorted his amusement, winning points from me. Herman puffed a big cloud of smoke, which could have meant anything. I let my remark ride and waited for a bid from the other players. They exchanged looks; the fit man got the nod from the fat man.

'It's something like an undercover operation,' Farrow said. 'Maybe there'll be a movie and maybe there won't be. I've written a script but I don't necessarily expect to see it make the screen.'

This was too much. I shook my head. 'I don't understand.'

Farrow leaned towards me across the table. 'We know all about you, Mr Browning. We know about your... comings and goings, shall we say.'

I remembered that I wasn't a spineless actor, ready to roll, belly-up, on the rug for a part. I was a private eye, licensed, bonded. I didn't have to take this shit. 'Who's we?'

'A very good question, yes,' Herman said. 'We is Mr Farrow and myself, certain other gentlemen and a man you may remember, one Mr Peter Groom, formerly of the FBI.'

The look on my face must have told them that I *did* remember. Groom was the G-man who'd suckered me into playing along with a bunch of crazy Klu Kluxers back in '38. He had a file on me that detailed the fillings in my teeth[20].

'Mr Groom's in military intelligence now,' Herman said smoothly. 'What is known, I believe, as a coming man.'

In '39, Groom had agreed not to act on any of the irregularities of my life—little matters such as illegal entry, bigamy, bankruptcy and the like—in return for my cooperation. 'We had a deal,' I said.

'You cannot deal with those people unless you have as much on them as they have on you, or more,' Herman said. 'I know. I bargained my way out of Germany in 1937. It was not easy, believe me.'

I wanted to say, 'So, why don't you make a movie out of that and leave me alone?' but I didn't. Instead, I listened to Farrow.

He was still fiddling with his cigarette, not lighting it. 'We have a strange situation here, Dick. The war's going well in some places, not so well in others. The strategy in the Pacific's obvious, especially to someone like you.'

I smoked and didn't say anything. I'd seen the maps in newspapers, and on the walls of the the real gung-ho types, bristling with pins. But it had never made any sense to me. I'm against war myself. The people who find it fun are crazy and need padded walls.

Farrow went on, 'We're island-hopping, of course, with the idea of getting a big enough force close enough to Japan to scare her into quitting. It takes time.'

That seemed safe enough to respond to. I nodded.

'You'd be aware of the propaganda value of movies?'

Another nod. Strong and silent. General Richard Kelly Browning, D.S.O., M.C. etc.

Farrow finally lit the cigarette. I learned that it was something he did when he got to the point. 'There's a movie going to be made about the liberation of the Philippines. It's going to hit the screens at exactly the same time as the men hit the beaches. It's going to give everyone at home a big lift.'

Herman snorted. 'Be honest with him, my friend. Can't you see that he is an intelligent man? The casualties in the Philippines will be very heavy and for the strike at Japan itself? Enormous. The film will stiffen the American spine.'

Coming from a guy whose spine was so encased in blubber it would have taken surgery to locate it, this was a bit rich. I felt like protesting, but I knew that what he was saying was the exact truth. Recruiting fell off after Gallipoli[21], and don't let anyone tell you different. I was losing the thread though.

'I thought this film was about Australia and... ah, New Guinea?'

Herman and Farrow exchanged the kinds of looks that indicate that half-truths are coming, if not outright lies. The smoke fug was building up in the room and

Farrow glanced at his watch. So time was a factor. I decided to play it cool. I removed my jacket and draped it over the back of my chair. I lit another cigarette. I had all the time in the world.

'Let me make it more clear to you,' Herman said. He ran his finger around the collar of his shirt, easing away some of the flab. 'To make this picture about the Philippines invasion, the work will have to start soon and it will take a long time. There will be liaison with the army and navy and air force.'

I was almost enjoying myself. 'And the marines. Don't forget the fighting marines.'

'Just so. The cooperation of the military is assured. They want the film for their reasons as much as we do for ours.'

'Money,' I said.

Farrow's voice cut through like a whip. 'No. To build a secure world. A Christian Europe, an American-influenced Pacific and South-east Asia.'

Another crazy trying to make the world safe for something nobody wanted very much. I took another look at Farrow. Those clear eyes, that firm jaw. I switched to Herman. Piggy eyes. Everything slack except his brain. I felt my own brain stretching, trying to follow what was going on. Herman came to the rescue.

'Hollywood has no secrets,' he said. 'If we start planning a film along the lines we have discussed, the enemy will hear of it most quickly. The military does not want that to happen.'

'So?' I said.

'So, an operation has been devised to deflect attention from the preparations for this film. While the plans are going ahead in secret...'

'I thought you said Hollywood had no secrets.'

'Touché,' Herman said. 'This is an exception. Another film will appear to be in the making. It concerns Australia and, what was the other place you mentioned?'

'New Guinea.'

'Yes. And the Dutch East Indies, I fancy. Mr Farrow has written a script; people will be assigned to the project. You will go to Australia. There will be publicity.'

'But no movie?'

Herman spread his pudgy hands. He wore jewelled rings on four fingers. 'This is Hollywood, Mr Browning. Who can say?'

'You've done some boxing, I believe,' Farrow said. 'So have I. This is a feint. It's an effective manoeuvre in the ring.'

I saw it all in a flash. Bobby Silk had ratted me out to these people. Maybe Groom had leaned on him in some way. It looked as if Bobby had started kicking over the traces, which would make him vulnerable. His wife wasn't an understanding woman. Whatever the reason, he'd served me up for this crazy scheme. I felt a rush of feeling—anger, disappointment, resentment at being used. Then I calmed down and thought about it. A spell of the star treatment. First-class hotels and travel. Expenses, no doubt. And no lines to learn, not really. If I had to go to Australia I could possibly sort a few things out, like a divorce if that was still required. I'd had no news of my family in almost twenty-five years. Maybe there'd be some change lying around to be picked up. On the other hand, flying over the Pacific in wartime...

'I'll think about it,' I said.

Herman stubbed out his cigar and brushed ash from his vest and trousers. Not much ash—he was a tidy smoker. Farrow did some neck-loosening exercises. Neither said anything; both looked suddenly uncomfortable.

'I'll let you know,' I said, just to keep the ball rolling.

Farrow shook his head. 'I don't think you have that luxury, Mr Browning,' he said.

16

The rest of the day was spent at what felt like the real thing—photograph session, wardrobe session, contract signing, delivery of a loose-leaf copy of the script and a press conference with Farrow and Herman sitting in and lying their back teeth out. All I had to do was look stern and masterful, like General Wilson Broderick, my character in the movie, who had a personal mission to remove every Japanese soldier from within a thousand miles of his beloved Australia. I'd be relying on American soldiers, airmen and sailors to help me and there was the rub—an antagonism between myself and US General Beau Elder. All a misunderstanding over a woman.

If it sounds thin, it was. The script was little more than an outline and anyone who tried to shoot it might end up with a comedy, if he was lucky. But that didn't matter. No-one outside the charmed circle ever saw the script, and the Hollywood press boys and girls knew their readers weren't interested in words on pages.

'Who're the stars, Mr Browning?'

I'd been primed for that one. 'Big names. I think I'm at liberty to say that Spencer Tracy is interested, and if he joins up he won't be playing Private Jones.'

That got a laugh.

'Why're you fronting now, Mr Browning?'

I kept the jaw up and the steely glint in the eye. 'I'm an Australian. I've been a soldier. It's my country... and yours.'

A good deal more of this. Some curly ones, such as about dates and methods of transport and whether I would actually have an Australian military rank, as Farrow had hinted. I fielded them as best I could, threw in the odd Australianism, and was desperate for a drink by late afternoon. It was all as phoney as a western sunrise, but you have to remember that this was wartime and that the war was the biggest news around. And in LA the combination of war news and movie news was irresistible. That was what the scheme rested on, of course. I scanned the ranks of the reporters, trying to spot the sceptic. The guy or woman who'd see through it and ask a question that would bring it all tumbling down. It didn't happen. They went away happy with notepads well covered and quotes from Herman like, 'There won't be a good Japanese movie until the United States is running the place.' That got a small hand.

At the end of the day I was told that my salary would be paid into my bank weekly and I was to stand by ready to go anywhere, anytime. There was another character in on the act by this stage—a tall, thin Texan named Loren Duke who spoke with an accent so thick I could hardly understand him. He muttered about being one of Peter Groom's boys, which made me take an instant dislike to him. He seemed to be the liaison man between the project and Paramount. Just to get under his skin, I pressured him to get me a daily pay envelope such as extras and bit players got.

'Not sure I can do that,' he drawled.

'Not sure I can give a good report on you to my old friend, Peter Groom, less'n you do.'

The use of Groom's name worried him and he went off to the administration building, leaving me to sit under a tree and smoke a cigarette and think how to milk this madness for all it was worth. I saw Bing Crosby walk by about thirty feet away and waved to him. He waved back although he didn't know me from Adam. The stars were like that; they met hundreds of people a day and instantly forgot ninety-nine per cent of them. They got so used to being acknowledged by people they didn't know that they just acknowledged back, without thinking. Providing you were in the right place, like inside the Paramount lot, or maybe in the betting ring at Santa Anita, you could have a bit of fun with them that way.

When Loren Duke came back he was wearing a smug expression. He handed me an envelope and a set of keys. 'This here's an advance on your salary, Mr Browning, and an apartment has been arranged for you at the Bryson.'

'I'm at the Wilcox.'

'Your bill has been paid and your things moved to the Bryson. I can run you over if you like.'

Loren had taken all the points. I accepted the envelope, feeling like a panhandler, and the keys. 'I've got my car here,' I said. 'I can find it.'

'Reckon I might tag along. Just to kinda see you settled in.'

I couldn't object to that, although I knew what lay behind it. As I say, Peter Groom knew everything about me, including the fact that my natural tendency, when things got not to my liking, was to leave town. In the car I checked the envelope. Two hundred clams. My salary was five hundred a week and, if you don't think it sounds like much, let me tell you it bought an awful lot in LA in 1943. I knew where the Bryson was, on Wiltshire Boulevard. I'd been to a party or two there in my acting days and, more recently, I'd guarded the furs and jewellery at a party thrown by Lillian Rose, who was celebrating the fact that she was leaving LA to go back to New York to work in the theatre. Half the drunks at the party swore they'd go with her. Three months later the play had closed and she was back.

I pulled into the car park beside the apartment house, showing my key to the attendant. Loren would have to shift for himself on the street. I wandered around to the front. The Bryson was a white stucco pile with a lot of tall date palms, some of them in pots as if they might be moved somewhere else if times got tough. There were marble entrance steps with two big stone lions on top of the columns, guarding them on either side. You went through an elaborate archway that looked like something out of *Ali Baba and the Forty Thieves*, into a big lobby with a thick blue carpet. The reception desk was a modest affair, hardly any gold inlay and only four telephones.

The Texan had caught up with me by the time the desk man had called a porter to show me to my apartment. He escorted us from the elevator on the sixth floor to the door of the apartment, which he unlocked with my key.

'Miss King hoped your things were arranged to suit you, Mr Browning,' the porter said.

That was enough to earn him a dollar from my envelope. I'd resolved not to spend a cent of my own money while this thing lasted. Everything from the Wilcox was here, including the ransacked files and torn clothes. God knows what Miss King must have thought of it, but then, God knows what Miss King thought about anything. It depended pretty much on who she really worked for, and that was anybody's guess.

Duke prowled through the place like it was him that was going to live there rather than me. It took him a while because a sixth-floor corner apartment in the Bryson wasn't a dog kennel—it had a big entrance hall with kitchen and bathroom off it, leading to a living room with a view towards MacArthur Park. There were two bedrooms. The master bedroom had its own bathroom; the smaller one had a three-quarter bed and writing desk. This was where they'd dumped my files. Sliding glass doors in the living room got you to a balcony which ran around the corner of the building. It was deep enough to hold several large pot-plants, a reclining lounge arranged to catch the morning sun, and a timber table and chair set at which you could take morning coffee or lay an evening meal with candles, according to your fancy.

'Looks okay,' Duke said.

'I'm glad you approve.'

'What happened to your stuff?' He nodded in the direction of the second bedroom. 'Looks like it went through a cotton gin.'

'Maybe you boys got to it,' I said. 'Maybe you were checking me out before giving me this important assignment.'

Duke shook his head. 'I don't think so. We're trained to go through clothes and sets of papers and leave not a one out of place.'

'Must show me how you do it one of these days. Meanwhile, I've had a long...'

'Sure, sure. I'll leave you to it. Did they say what time you were wanted in the morning?'

'No.'

'I'll find out and give you a call.'

'That's not necessary. I...'

'Just obeying orders, Mr Browning. I sure do want to get that good report you spoke about.'

Duke ambled out of the apartment with a smile on his thin face. He left the door open and I had to walk all that way down the passage to close it. Somehow, I thought Loren Duke had taken the points on day one of our relationship.

The telephone brought me out of an uneasy sleep. I'd taken off my tie and shoes and stretched out on the bed just to get the feel of it. That was at around six o'clock. Now it was dark and the phone was ringing. I leapt off the bed and headed for the living room before I remembered where I was. I flopped back and reached for the phone on the bedside table.

'Browning.'

'Richard.'

The voice was breathless and sounded panicky, but I would have recognised it anywhere.

'May Lin. What the hell...'

'I am in terrible danger. I cannot think of anyone else to help me. Please.'

'Where are you?'

'I'm in a bar on Vermont—the Manhattan. I can't pay my tab or for this call. Please, come and get me.'

'How did you know I was here? How did you know my number? *I* don't even know my number.'

'I'll explain. Richard, please. Come now.'

There I was, in a very nice apartment, big bed, well-stocked kitchen and refrigerator. I forgot to mention that. There were flowers in vases, food and drink in the kitchen. I'd been too tired to care. I'd had a couple of hours sleep and felt almost perky. I did what any red-blooded man would do.

'Stay right there, honey,' I said. 'I'm on my way.'

I meant it too. But not every red-blooded man has a Smith & Wesson .38 to help him along. I strapped it on, climbed back into my clothes, shrugged on the trench coat that had the lining ripped out of it and left the apartment. I had a heavy stubble, no tie and the stairway lights in the Bryson were dim. Outside, there was no moon and not much in the way of streetlights. I could hardly see the stone lions on the tops of their pillars, but I gave them a growl anyway. I'd been tricked and pampered; I was sober, rested and had a pistol in my armpit. I was also remembering a sinuous, ivory body that writhed and thrashed and moaned and was young and innocent one moment, and old and full of sin the next. I was in a very dangerous condition.

The Manhattan was only walking distance away. Nowadays in LA that's fifty yards; *then* it was quarter of a mile. I walked along Wiltshire in the direction of the Brown Derby where I'd paid a call with Pete McVey. It seemed like a lifetime ago. I made the turn onto Vermont and couldn't help looking around for unwanted company. Communists, Nationalists, FBI, Military Intelligence? Who could say? The traffic was light and the sidewalks were almost deserted. A woman walked her dog; a guy in a tux asked me the way to the Park Plaza. I told him, pointed. He was very drunk and I doubted he'd make it. The only suspicious-looking character on the street was me.

The Manhattan was one of those fake New York joints that LA specialised in, then and now. I haven't been in New York for twenty years. I've often wondered if it has fake LA joints but, since almost all of LA is fake somewhere else, it's hard to imagine how. The bar was dimly lit with a neon Schlitz beer sign in the window. The 'l' wasn't illuminated; I'd been told the signs could be made that way.

The place was dark and smoky inside. Not many people—Monday night crowd, professional drinkers and people congratulating themselves on having got through the first day of another week. May Lin was in a booth. She had an empty glass in front of her and was smoking a cigarette. I laid a five on the bar and told the barman to bring two of whatever she'd been drinking across to the booth. I took off my coat and slid in opposite her. It's hard to describe tired Oriental eyes, but hers were. Her face was pale and drawn and her make-up had just about faded away. Some brown hair straggled loose from the tight bun on the top of her head. She was wearing the clothes I'd seen her in last and they were wrinkled as well as all wrong for this time and place. She still looked beautiful.

'Thank you for coming, Richard.'

I shook out a cigarette and lit it. Hers had an inch or so to go before it joined the ten or more of the same brand in the ashtray. She'd had quite a wait.

'You'll want explanations,' she said.

'Uh huh.'

The drinks came—bourbon on the rocks. The waiter looked relieved that someone with some money had turned up. I took a drink, smoked and waited.

'I found out from your agent where you were living now. Also the telephone number.'

That could play. A bit late now to check, but let it pass. 'How did you know I was still alive? The last you saw me I was having my head shape changed by a blackjack.'

She gave an involuntary jerk and took a pull on her drink. 'Yes. It was terrible. They hurt me too.'

I wasn't going to buy that, not just yet. 'You haven't answered the question, May Lin.'

She lifted her chin and looked directly at me. Unless she was a better actress than any woman for a hundred miles around (which was always possible), she'd been through something that had scared her and worn her down. The hard, brittle surface she'd worn on our previous meetings had chipped away. She looked vulnerable, as if there was another, softer person struggling to emerge. She drank a little bourbon and lit one of my cigarettes.

'My uncle told me about your visit to the Reverend Moon's church. Nothing happens in the Chinese community that he doesn't know about.'

Plausible again. I could feel myself wanting to believe her, and wanting more than that. If you've ever met an old lover, after a gap of some years, and felt a quick recognition of signals, a quick cut to the chase as they say in Hollywood, you'll know how it was. Not that there was much of a gap—we'd been making love about eighty hours before. I reached across the damp, ash-strewn surface and took her hand. Her long slender fingers entwined in mine and I felt a shudder run through her.

'What happened to you, May Lin?' I said. 'What's this all about?'

17

She kissed my hand and we left the bar. She began to talk, but not about herself. I got some of the story on the walk back to the Bryson and the rest of it in bed. May Lin said that she was an agent of the Chinese Nationalist government and a colleague of Sue Feng, Hart Sallust's wife. According to Sue Feng, Sallust had revealed in a drunken row that he knew details of the plans to secure the Sun, Moon and Stars and the other treasures and he threatened to write about it. Sue Feng swore that Sallust had not learned this from her and she did not know what his source of information could have been. She reported the alarming facts to a committee of Kuomintang supporters in California, one of whom was Singapore Sam.

I listened to this and then explained to May Lin that McVey and I had learned something about these matters from Reverend Moon. I filled her in on that and she became even more willing to talk.

'I was given the job of getting close to Sallust and finding out what he was writing about and what his source of information was.'

'How did you manage that?'

We'd made love after sharing a bath and several glasses of champagne. May Lin wasn't the innocent or the tigress this time, more the languid, yielding kind and the lovemaking had been very good. One thing I had done was check on her neck wound. It was genuine and she had a few more scratches and bruises, as well. We were under the sheets with our bodies just touching. I was still doubtful and alert for any reaction that might indicate an evasion or a lie. She lay perfectly still.

'Joe Herman is a Kuomintang sympathiser. As soon as this trouble started he made the agreement with Sallust. The one you could scarcely believe.'

'Right,' I said. 'Sallust must have thought he'd died and gone to screenwriters' heaven.'

May Lin shook her head. 'No. He was very frightened. Of everything. Anyway, it was Herman who arranged for me to work with him.'

I tried to keep my voice free of complaint or reproof. 'You told us you didn't find out what was going on. Was that true?'

'Yes. Absolutely true. The man was terrified. He talked about a story in the most general terms—heroes and villains, treasures, yes, he talked about treasures, but in a joking way. He referred to the books of Robert Louis Stevenson. He said he was related to him.'

I hadn't read them, but I knew the titles. They were given out as school prizes at Dudleigh and I'd seen the swots and arse-lickers clutching the leather-bound volumes.

'*Treasure Island, Kidnapped*,' I said.

She gave me a respectful glance and I gave thanks for my good memory. 'Yes. He was drunk almost all the time and terribly afraid. He talked about going to Mexico, but he didn't have a passport or any money until he wrote the script and he was unable to do that.'

'Did he do any writing?'

'No. None. After he'd passed out at night I searched, but I never found anything.'

I'd done some searching too—while she was still in the bath. She had no weapons in her purse or clothes and the door was locked. She was tired and almost asleep. I might not have trusted her completely, but I had no fear of her either.

'May Lin,' I said again, 'what happened to you?'

She told me that the men who'd stopped us on the road had gagged and blindfolded her and taken her further along the coast before turning inland. She'd heard the waves for an hour or so and then the road got rough and she realised she was in hill country. They'd taken her to a house and locked her in a bare basement room.

'It was cold and I was very frightened, but they didn't do anything to me.'

'No questions? No threats?'

'No. Nothing. It must have been a big house but I was below ground level and didn't see anything. I could hear movement above me but a long way off. It was dark and cold and there was only a cot with one blanket to sleep on. They'd taken everything from me. I didn't even have my cigarettes. I banged on the door and yelled for water, but nothing happened.'

I put my arm around her shoulders and pulled her closer to me. 'Then what?'

'I slept for a while. When I woke up there was some food and some milk. I was ravenous. I ate it all and drank the milk. Then I went back to sleep almost straight away. It must have had something in it. I woke up with a terribly sore throat and a headache. There was someone banging on the door. A voice outside told me to put the blindfold back on. He said if I didn't or tried to cheat he'd kill me. I did it.'

'So would I,' I said. 'Did you recognise the voice?'

She thought for a minute before shaking her head. 'No, not exactly.'

'What do you mean?'

'I know they were Chinese. You can tell. When I had the blindfold on they came in and took me up some steps and out of the house. I could tell that it was daylight but the blindfold was very thick and they tightened it. I couldn't see anything. I could tell that we were in the woods. There were good smells, some I sort of recognised. Flowers, maybe. But I don't know anything about flowers, and I was still very scared.'

'What was being said?'

'Nothing. I was just prodded and pushed. Not too roughly. It's funny—I got the feeling that they were afraid of hurting me but would if they had to. That was scary, too.'

She stopped to light a cigarette. She'd had a pack at the bar, but no purse and no money. She could see that I was looking for holes in her story but she didn't fly off the handle. 'Ask,' she said.

'How did you get back to LA?'

'They dropped me in Venice, near my uncle's place. They gave me five dollars. I don't know why.'

It was all weird enough to be true, but I was still unconvinced. 'You didn't go to Sam's though,' I said. 'You haven't changed your clothes or anything.'

'No. The first thing I did was buy cigarettes. I'm a terrible smoker. Not so heavy, but very hooked.'

'Me too.'

'I was afraid to go to my uncle's.'

'Why?'

'I don't know. Just a feeling that it was not safe. I get such feelings sometimes and I always trust them. My uncle wanted me to come to him but I refused. I asked him about you, and he told me you and Mr McVey had been to see Reverend Moon. I phoned your agent. This was all from that bar. I phoned you and I had no money left.'

It all sounded kosher or, if it wasn't, I was too tired and too sexually contented to care. I smoked another cigarette and drank the last of the wine. I gave up thinking about Tan and Moon and Hart Sallust and the Sun, Moon and Stars. I had nothing new to think about on the matter anyway. May Lin snuggled down close to me and her breathing became regular and soft. I drifted off to sleep, holding her slender, sweet-smelling body in my arms.

I came wide awake about five hours later with my mind clear and a piece of information I'd forgotten firmly slotted back into place. I sat up and stared at the ribbons of light forming around the window.

'His sister!'

May Lin grabbed at the sheet I'd pulled up with me and came awake too. 'What?'

'His sister. Hart has a sister. She's a librarian. He used to go to her place to try to dry out. Chandler told me that if Sallust wanted to hide anything he'd do it where he hides the booze.'

'Chandler who?'

I told her about Raymond Chandler. She wasn't impressed. I guess she had a reason to feel jaundiced about writers, but she was still keen to press on with her job and glad to have a lead.

'Where does she live? We must check this out.'

I scratched at my stubble. 'Truth is, I don't remember where she lives. LA someplace. And I don't even know her name. I guess she's Sallust's half-sister. She's got a different name. I've heard it, but I don't remember.'

She thumped the pillow angrily. 'You must! It's important.'

'I know. I'll try. But I can't do anything about it today.' I told her about *South Pacific Showdown*. I didn't tell her that the whole thing was a charade. I pointed to the bound script that was lying on the floor. It had been on the bed before we put the bed to better use. I explained that I had appointments all day—costume, script discussion, medical examination. She picked up the script and leafed through it.

'Not very good,' she said.

I shrugged. 'Farrow wrote it and he's the director. I guess he can do what he likes with it in the shooting. They say *Casablanca* didn't really have a script at all.'

'Do you want to do this, Richard?'

'Sure. It's good money. You don't think I usually live in the Bryson, do you? I had one room with a Murphy bed in the Wilcox until today... yesterday.'

'I see. So I must go on with this alone?'

I thought about Hank and his rifle and Charles Tan and his pliers. May Lin had got to me. She looked fresh and lovely first thing in the morning, which is a rare thing in a woman. She depended on me and I didn't want to let her down—a rare feeling for me. I kissed her and threw the script across the room. 'You don't have to do it alone. We'll do it together. It'll just take a bit longer because of all this movie stuff, but I'll find the time.'

'What about Mr McVey?'

'Bobby Silk's fired him. He's not interested in Sallust anymore, he says. But Pete's still working on it in Frisco. When he gets back, we'll talk to him.'

She asked me what Pete was doing and I remembered—he was in Frisco to look for Sue Feng. I told her. May Lin shook her head. 'She won't tell him anything, even if he finds her. Which I doubt. The sister is a better lead if you can come up with her name.'

'I'm confused,' I said. 'I need a shower and a bucket of coffee.'

We took the shower together. I started to make the coffee while May Lin got a carton of eggs out of the refrigerator. She confessed that cooking was one of her passions and that she made the best scrambled eggs in California.

'That's great,' I said. I put some money on the bench. 'Maybe you'd like to poke your head out just long enough to get something for dinner. I want to have it here with you.'

I was stunned by my own actions and what my words implied and so was she. We were in the breakfast nook.

The space was filled with sunlight; May Lin was wearing one of my shirts and I had an old silk dressing gown with a faded Chinese pattern wrapped around me. I dropped the filter paper into the sink and she broke an egg all over the serving bench. We both got clear of the small table and embraced fiercely.

'Do you realise what you just said?' I could feel the movement of her lips against my chest.

'Yes,' I said. 'I love you, May Lin.'

18

It was true, God help me. Everything about her delighted me and I wanted to learn still more and get closer to her in every way. I hadn't had a lot of luck with women and they hadn't had much with me. This was different. This was mutual, and the dangerous business we were involved in only helped to stoke the fire.

We abandoned breakfast and went back to bed.

Later, Loren Duke phoned to say that he was coming by to pick me up for a series of meetings and appointments that would keep me busy for the whole day. I thought it would be tricky explaining to May Lin why I couldn't tell Duke to get lost, but she didn't seem to care.

'I'll stay here and get some rest,' she said. 'I wish I had some clothes, though.'

'Where do you live?'

'Venice. I've got an apartment near my uncle's club. But I can't go there. I'm... afraid.'

I got the address from her and she told me there was a key under a potted cactus by the door. I said I'd go by and pick up some clothes. I also said I'd try to remember about Hart Sallust's sister.

Suddenly, May Lin snapped her fingers under my nose. 'What's her name?'

I smiled and shook my head. 'Sometimes works, but not this time. Hart did some movies for Paramount.

Maybe if I talk to some people on the lot the penny'll drop.'

May Lin looked puzzled. I explained the expression. She laughed and kissed me. 'I'd like to go to Australia,' she said.

'It's being talked about in connection with this picture. Maybe you could come.'

'I have some relatives who went out there in the gold rush days,' she said. 'When did your people go.'

'Earlier,' I said. 'In the convict days.'

That day at Paramount and around Hollywood in the company of Loren Duke was pretty much like the day before. I was in something of a love haze and didn't take a lot of it in. I remember being fitted for a uniform and an Australian named Bruce advising the wardrobe people about the medals and insignia General Broderick Wilson would wear. I had lunch in the Brown Derby on Vine Street. Bette Davis was at the table but I didn't get to talk to her. She hardly talked to anyone in the room. She was constantly being paged and the telephone kept appearing and she did her talking to it. Still, the impression was created that we were involved in a project together and impressions were what this job, and the Brown Derby, were all about.

Back at the lot there was a session with some East Coast journalists and then I pleaded a headache. Loren Duke looked at me sceptically. 'How old are you, Browning?'

Our relationship had deteriorated steadily so that we were now scarcely on civil terms.

'Older than I look,' I said. 'I want to go to the commissary for a cup of tea.'

'You a juicer?'

I stared at him and didn't answer.

'You Aussies lace your tea with rum, don't you?'

I thought about tea-drinking in Australia—the ladies of Mosman and Brighton, the wowsers in every city and town. 'Where the hell did you get that idea?'

'I read some books by this guy Upfield. Great books about the outback. The guys are always spiking their tea with rum. Even in the morning[22].'

'That's what comes from reading books,' I said. 'I want to go to the commissary. Fact is I hate tea, but if I'm going to Australia to play this bloody general I'm going to have to get used to it again.'

Duke couldn't argue with that. He had a quick conference with Patty King and they found me a free hour. What I really wanted to do was drop in at the writer's table in the commissary. This was in a small ante-room to the main feeding area and I'd seen it in operation when I'd been a bit player at Paramount. The writers had long lunches there, sometimes extending into the late afternoon. There was a lot of laughing and horsing around and I remember Hart Sallust saying that he got some of his best ideas and best lines right there.

I got rid of Duke and went to the commissary by myself. The place was very quiet, a few people sitting around talking quietly over coffee and cigarettes. There were four men in the writers' section—one was Harry Tugend, who was renowned for his gossipy sense of humour; two others I didn't know, and Billy Morgan.

Billy was a pale, plump Brooklynite who'd worked as a rewrite man on *Kid Galahad*, a writing odd-job man as I'd been an acting odd-jobber. We'd had a few drinks and poker games together. He was going nowhere at his own good speed and didn't care who knew it. He was a boozer, a sports fan and a poker fiend, occupations also indulged in by Hart Sallust.

You only went into that room if you were invited, and you only got invited if someone thought you might have something witty to say. I wasn't renowned for my wit but it must've been a slow time because Billy beckoned me in.

'Say, Dick,' he said, 'they tell me you got a lightweight out in Australia could take Beau Jack. That so?'

Sporting news was one of the few things I kept up with. I nodded hello to Tugend and the others. 'That's right,' I said, 'name of Vic Patrick.'

Morgan's pale eyebrows went up. 'Irish, eh?'

'Yeah,' I said. 'Like Jack McGurn. His real name's Lucca[23]. He's an eye-talian.'

It wasn't very funny, but it was enough to get a snigger from Tugend and a glance from the two men he was talking with. I sat down next to Morgan. 'Listen, Billy,' I said, 'have you seen anything of Hart Sallust lately?'

Morgan shook his head. 'Naw. He owe you money?'

'Not exactly. How well do you know him?'

'Well enough to ask that question. Hart's okay except that he can't hold his liquor. He's flopped at my place a few times.'

'Did you ever meet his sister?'

'Sure. Swell woman. She picked him up one time, took him to her place to dry out.'

'Wouldn't happen to know her name and where she lives?'

He shook his head. 'Was a while back. I might remember if you give me time. Tell me about this Patrick.'

Morgan was playing the old Hollywood game of scratch my back. Maybe there was a match being set up between Patrick and Beau Jack and he was hoping to get some money down at the right odds. I told him that Patrick was welterweight and lightweight champion of Australia, that he was a southpaw with a long jaw and a punch that could stop a man cold.

'Don't like the sound of the jaw,' Billy said.

'He's had over forty fights and won nearly all of them by KO. No-one's tagged him yet.'

Billy nodded, got out a little black notebook and scribbled something, then he flicked over a few pages. He grinned and read, 'Beatrice Trudeau. Phone number in Pasadena, 6598.'

I snapped my fingers. 'That's it. Hart called her Beat, and he said his mother married a Frenchman after his Dad kicked.'

'That right? Well, she's not exactly your type, Dick, less'n you've got religion lately.'

'What do you mean?'

Tugend and his companions pushed their chairs back and Morgan did the same. I guess he didn't want to be the last writer to go back to work. I grabbed his sleeve. He looked alarmed. He might write about tough guys beating each other up in the alley, but even the smell of the real thing worried him. He pulled his arm away. 'Take it easy.'

'Billy, tell me what you meant. There could be a buck in it for you.'

'Aw, Hart told me his sister was in close with some church or other. Some Chinese Christian malarkey.'

He gave me a salute and followed the others out of the commissary. Violating all the rules, I stayed sitting at the writers' table. I lit a cigarette and wanted a drink. I was still sitting there when Loren Duke came to get me to watch screen tests for other actors in the picture that wasn't scheduled or written and would never be made.

A private eye who can't match up a phone number with an address isn't going to get anywhere. The cops have a book that makes the match and various other people buy the information from the cops. I knew a guy who had a copy of the match book and I phoned him just before I left Paramount.

'A ten spot in your mailbox tomorrow,' I said. 'Beatrice Trudeau, Pasadena 6598.'

'That's 129 Shakespeare. You want me to spell it?'

'You'd charge extra,' I said, 'and probably get it wrong. Thanks.'

'Just make sure you say it ten times tomorrow, Dick.'

I finally shook Duke off by telling him I was too tired to grab a beer. All I wanted to do was go to bed, I said.

'I hear you've got company at the Bryson.'

'That's right. An adult female. Any law against that?'

He shook his head and sighed. 'Nope. This town being the way it is, I'd say I downright approve. Call you in the morning.'

I drove to Venice to the address May Lin had given me. The apartment block was standard Californian, which is to say Spanish with some of the frills missing. It was three storeys high, built of brick, painted white, with a flat roof and a series of small balconies and landings reached by stairways running up the outside of the building. There were white stones and palm trees in small courtyards at ground level, and every apartment had a car parking space allotted to it in a big, open-fronted garage at the back of the building. It was a classy place and I wouldn't have minded living there myself. You'd be able to see the water from the higher levels, and those balconies looked like nice spots to catch a bit of sun and sip a few cold ones.

I wasn't so seduced by it as to be careless, though. I drove around the block a few times, noting the cars parked in the streets and the people moving around on the street. Nothing suspicious. May Lin had apartment ten and there was no car in her slot. I parked my Olds there, backing it in so that I could take off quickly if need be. It didn't seem likely. Venice is different from most of LA, or was then. The place gives off a relaxed feeling, as if you can leave the pressures behind you on the road and come down here to a more comfortable way of life. I was regretting that I'd ever left it. Then I remembered the circumstances —the threats of death or worse[24]—and I shed the feeling.

I scouted around in the courtyards until I found the steps leading to apartment ten. It was on the second storey, at the front and would command a respectable water view. I couldn't guess at the rent—well above mine at the Wilcox, maybe around what someone was paying at the Bryson. Weird thoughts. In cheap places you get snoopers, bored people with nothing on their minds so they pry into other people's business. Good for investigators, not so good for the citizenry. In better locations you get privacy. May Lin had it here. There were a few lights on in the apartment block, but no fluttering curtains, no inquisitive eyes. The cactus sprouted just where May Lin said it would and I snagged my sleeve, just as she said I would if I wasn't careful. I slid the key out and opened the door.

I liked the smell—incense, perfume, the smell of a woman. I went down a spiral staircase into the living room which was big and square with large windows and a lot of pot-plants. I switched on the light. Good carpet, settee, a couple of chairs, some cushions and magazines scattered about. I'd been right—through the window I could see the dark ocean rolling in. After the long day I was ready for a beer and I found a couple of bottles of a brand I didn't recognise in the refrigerator. I uncapped one and drank—thin and sweetish, but not too bad. There was wine in the fridge and a selection of the sort of food a person living alone can whip up quickly. I liked that, the confirmation that May Lin lived here alone.

I drank most of the beer while sitting in a chair in the living room and looking out at the sea. It was philosophy time—a feeling that comes over me about once every ten years. I had an impulse to take stock, to review my life's successes and mistakes and wonder if I could cut down on the one and build up on the other. As usual, no decision. I looked at the paintings on the walls which were pleasing—about as far as I go in art appreciation. I sighed and put down the bottle. There was only one bedroom. I opened the door and turned on the light. Double bed, unfussy room. Built-in closets with a full-length mirror. I heard a sound, felt a movement, saw something and then I was hit from behind not too far from the place I'd been hit before. The room spun.

19

It was the mirror that saved me. I'd got just enough of a glimpse of danger to duck and reduce the force of the blow to my head. I went down but I wasn't unconscious. I lay doggo while Charles Tan, aka Mr Brown, rubbed the side of his meaty hand that had delivered the rabbit punch.

'Mr Browning,' he said. His voice oozed self-satisfaction. 'We meet again. So pleased.'

He reached down to grab the front of my shirt. I remembered the pliers; fear and panic sharpened my reflexes. I rolled away from him and reached behind me for the .38 in its holster lying against my spine. I got a clean grip and a quick draw. I had the gun up and cocked and pointing at his gut before he could make another move.

'Hey?' he said.

I was too scared to do anything other than what I did. I got to my feet and hit him above the left ear with the barrel of the gun. He sagged and I hit him again. I wanted him down and not moving. His knees touched the floor and I almost repeated the dose, but his dark, slanted eyes rolled back and I stopped in midswing. I was woozy and still very afraid. I looked at him, collapsed and still beside the bed and felt sick. *Don't spoil it, Dick,* I thought, *keep it classy.*

I waited until I was sure he was out; then I put the gun on the bed within reach and took off his tie.

I pinioned his wrists and strapped them tight. After that I felt more secure. He wore braces. I unfastened them and used them to tie his ankles. I remembered what he'd said about trussing a person so that any movement caused strangulation, but I wasn't that much of a tough guy. I went into the kitchen, wet a dishcloth and opened another bottle of beer. Back in the bedroom I took a long suck on the bottle and felt the pain in my head settle down into a dull ache. I squeezed the cloth over Tan's head and let the water run into his eyes, nose and mouth. He spluttered and I slapped him across the face with the cloth. I was tough enough for that.

'Wake up, Charlie,' I said. 'Sore head?'

He groaned.

'Mine was, too. Still is, a bit. We're sharing a lot of experiences, aren't we? I'm pleased to see you again as well.'

He glowered at me.

I shook my head. 'Maybe you're not as pleased as you thought. Maybe you'd like to help things along by telling me what you're doing here.'

'You don't know what you're getting yourself into, Browning,' Tan said. 'You're way out of your depth, Limey.'

'Australian,' I said. 'I think I've met some of your folks out there—market gardeners and such, nice, quiet people. I think they'd be ashamed of you, Charlie. What're you doing in May Lin's apartment?'

'She's my little sweetie pie. I was waiting for her to come back so I could fuck her again.'

I hit him hard with the wet cloth. It left a red mark across his smooth face.

'You've bought every woman you've ever had,' I said. 'You haven't got a nice enough personality to get 'em any other way. But you interest me, Charlie. How'd you know not to come back to the cabin?'

He sneered at me. 'Like I say, Browning, you don't know shit. I found that out when I put the pliers to you. You'd have sung like Nelson Eddy if you'd had anything to give. I saw your pal on the track above the cabin. Hank was just about useless anyway. I thought I'd leave it in the lap of the gods. It didn't make any difference to me which way it came out.'

That was cold-blooded enough for anyone. Suddenly, I felt very uneasy around Mr Tan, even if he was tied up. I had the feeling that if our positions were reversed, I might go sailing out the window down on to the hard white stones in the courtyard. I drank some beer and reached for the gun. No-one's ever praised my acting, but sometimes we rise above ourselves. I put the .38 up against Tan's right eyeball, under the lid.

'May Lin's my girl,' I said. 'I'm in love with her and your boys gave her a rough time. I don't like that. There's a cop in Santa Monica named Martingdale who's not too happy about the way things went down in that cabin. He'd like to tidy up a little. You're a dirty guy, Charlie, and I get the feeling Martingdale doesn't like Orientals. Then there's Singapore Sam, who doesn't like his niece being abducted. Everyone'd be happy for me to serve you up on a plate.'

'You wouldn't have the guts,' Tan said.

I removed the pistol from his eye socket. 'I'm not sure myself,' I said. 'I killed a lot of men in the war, but I was a sniper. Up close might be different, but somehow I don't think so.'

The red mark stood out more boldly as his face lost colour. 'You don't know what you're doing.'

I grabbed a pillow off the bed and rammed it up against the side of his head. I jammed the gun against it. 'I've got a feeling I can do it, Charlie. Tell me what I don't understand. That's the second time you've said that. Enlighten me. Convince me. I just might leave you alive here and send your mother and brother to get you. I just might.'

The mention of his mother and brother seemed to take something out of him. His eyes dropped closed for a moment and he looked older and tired. There was a trickle of blood coming from above his ear. It ran down his face and wet the collar of his linen shirt. He noticed and grimaced.

'I'll say this for you, Browning,' he muttered, 'you've got more balls than I gave you credit for. But take my advice. Stay out of this. I'm just about ready to give it the big miss myself.'

I wiped the neck of the beer bottle and put it to his mouth. He took a long swig. 'We're talking about the Sun, Moon and Stars, are we, Charlie?'

He nodded and winced as his head hurt. 'Yeah, I was going to have one last throw at it. Thought the May Lin broad might know something.'

'Why so negative? You're a tough guy, ex-marine. You swing a mean pair of pliers. This stuff's worth a fortune. You wouldn't just walk away from it.'

'When a piss-ant like you can take me, it's time I did. But that's not it. Look, I'll tell you everything I know about it and you let me go. Okay? No Santa Monica cops, no Reverend Moon, nothing. Okay?'

I nodded. 'If you convince me.'

It took about half an hour, another bottle of beer and some more gentle use of the dishcloth. I wiped the blood away and cleaned the cut on his head, which was more than he would have done for me. At first, he said he wanted a hand free to smoke. That he couldn't talk without tobacco. I laughed at him and he talked anyway. He said he'd become aware of the plan to get the Chinese treasures to America by overhearing conversations between his mother and brother and other members of their organisation.

'They're going to move the stuff to Taiwan. Then get it across the Pacific to the States. I don't know where and I don't know when, but I was expecting to find out. I heard that Sallust's wife had spilled a few beans and Sallust was writing about it. That's why I snatched you and May Lin.'

'Not Sallust? You haven't got him?'

'Would I have fucked around with you if I had him? No, that's the problem. There's someone else interested and it's someone very heavy.'

'What d'you mean?'

'My car got burnt out early this morning. My place got tossed.'

'Like you tossed mine?'

'Worse, much worse. And my woman was roughed up bad.'

'Where were you?'

He sighed. 'I was on an opium toot. I tell you, I got problems, Browning. I was looking for this big score to get me clear, but I think it's more likely to get me dead. I've had enough.'

I gave him a cigarette then, taking it out of his mouth to let him exhale and putting it back to let him suck the smoke down deep. He looked like a man at the end of his tether. I believed his story.

I thought aloud. 'Sue Cheng, Sallust's wife, says she didn't know where he got his information from. Have you got any clues on that?'

Tan thought about it. 'Maybe from the guy who grabbed him. Maybe he figured Sallust was a big-mouth and had to be shut up.'

'Maybe,' I said. 'If that's it we probably can't expect to see much more of old Hart.'

The beer and tobacco had put some toughness back into Charlie. He shrugged, as far as you can shrug when you're tied up like that. 'Who gives a shit?'

'I do,' I said.

'You're a fool. Let it go. Let the crazy Chink bastards jerk each other around.'

He was a very angry man with a lot of problems, as he'd said. I wondered whether I could just release him. I wondered about a lot of things. I got up off the bed and stubbed out the cigarette he'd only half smoked.

'Hey,' he said. 'What're you doing?'

'I came here to get some clothes for May Lin,' I said. 'Your boys left her a bit bedraggled.'

'My boys,' he spat out. 'Those punks. When they found out she was Sam's niece they couldn't get rid of her quick enough.'

I tucked the .38 back in its holster and made sure there was nothing sharp around that Charlie could get his hands on. I lifted a corner of the bed and put it down between his trussed legs, just above the ankles. He lay there and cursed me. I opened a closet and took down a selection of clothes—a couple of dresses, some slacks on hangers, a light coat. 'This'll take a few trips,' I said. 'I'll take this lot down to my car and think about what to do with you, Charlie.'

'We had a deal!'

'Did we?' I opened drawers in a cabinet beside the bed until I found the underwear. I grabbed a handful—all black silk—and felt a sexual shudder run through me. I was anxious to see May Lin in black silk underwear while I told her what a hero I'd been. I stuffed the frilly things in a pocket of the coat and went out of the bedroom.

I struggled up the staircase with the clothes, along the passageway, then braced myself against the wall as I put the door on the latch. Then it was out into the soft night and down the steps to my car. I dropped the stuff across the roof and lit a cigarette. I had to think what to do about Tan. I smoked and thought but nothing came. I got the car key out of my pocket and, just as I was unlocking the door, all hell broke loose. The night quiet was blown apart by sirens and gunfire. I dropped to the ground and pulled out my gun. My breath was coming in short gusts. I'd had enough action for one night. I could hear tyres screaming; blue lights winked from the road as glass broke and people shouted. I kept low. But the centre of the activity moved down the street and I was left panting on the gravel, my gun hand wet with sweat and a pair of black silk panties on top of my head.

Doors were banging and windows were opening in the houses and apartments along the street. A pair of dogs howled long, mournful off-key notes at each other from either side of the road. It was an unusual event for that part of town at that time of night, but not unknown. Black hopheads sometimes cruised down from east LA looking for trouble and the occasional desperado took a crack at the occasional liquor store on Venice Boulevard. Nothing to do with me. I put the gun back and stowed the clothes in the car.

I strolled back into May Lin's apartment thinking that it would be nice to spend a night or two here with her when this mess was all over. I was just about ready to bail out, like Charles Tan. Why not leave the whole thing alone? Convince May Lin that the secret agent stuff was for the birds. Maybe take her to Australia where she could meet some of the people in Little Collins Street and Dixon Street and we could all sit around over the chop suey. I looked into the kitchen wondering if there was anything here May Lin would need. I couldn't think of anything except maybe a few bottles of the beer which, I'd decided, was a fairly potent drop.

I hauled the last two out of the refrigerator along with a bottle of Californian white wine, and set them on the bench.

I checked the living room over with the same question in mind. Maybe she'd like some of her records. There was a phonograph in the Bryson apartment and a little dance music seemed like a good idea. I flicked through the discs, but it was all opera and classical stuff. I pulled out the 'Emperor Concerto' by Beethoven and 'Bolero' by Ravel which I vaguely remembered having heard and recalled because they had a bit of life. I made some noise doing this and I wondered why Charlie was so quiet. Surely he should have been showing a little interest in my state of mind. He must have heard the shots and sirens through the window too. Why so quiet, Charlie?

I unshipped the .38 and slid along the wall to the bedroom door, cocking an ear at the hinges, but hearing nothing. I waited. Still nothing. I couldn't stand there all night. I crouched and sneaked a look around the door. Charles Tan lay where I'd left him, his bound legs pinioned by the bed. The only difference was that his head was at an odd angle to the rest of him. Not a natural angle—the sort of angle that means your neck has been broken and you're dead.

20

I wouldn't say I panicked, but I wasn't icy cool either. I took one good look at Tan. His eyes were wide open in surprise but whoever had killed him must have found the job easy. I felt a stab of guilt and then thought what Charlie might have done to me if I hadn't got lucky. I remembered the pliers. I swept a look around the room, noticed nothing, and jerked open a closet to get another handful of clothes—skirts and blouses this time. I slung them over my arm and went out of the bedroom without looking again at Tan.

I picked up the records in the living room and the bottles in the kitchen and left the apartment. I was on the steps to the ground level before I realised what a sitting duck I made—arms full of clothes and junk, gun in holster, blood pressure high. But nothing happened. I made it to the car and threw the stuff inside. I forced myself to take three deep breaths before starting the engine. I didn't need a flooded motor. All I needed was to be out of there. The motor caught and I revved it gently and took off smartly, thankful that I'd backed the car in. There was no movement in the courtyard or the street. All the excitement seemed to have died down. I was five miles from Venice, on the way back to Hollywood, before I remembered that, as well as leaving a corpse, I'd left my fingerprints on a dozen record sleeves, several cigarette butts and three beer bottles back in May Lin's apartment.

If I'd ever had any thought of going to Pasadena to talk to Hart Sallust's sister that night, the events in Venice cancelled them out. I was frightened. Someone had cashed Charles Tan's chips in the most butal and ruthless manner. I guessed that the fracas in the street had driven him off, otherwise... I didn't like to think about it. Plus, I was worried on May Lin's account. What if Tan had spun some lying story about her? Or me? At the very least, I needed an ally. Where was McVey?

I drove back to Wiltshire and looked the area over carefully before putting the Olds into the car park. I took a small selection of the clothes up to the apartment, mostly the underwear, so that I could keep one hand free for the .38. The desk man had gone off duty; the stairs and corridors were dark and still. I jumped at my own shadow as I moved along to my door. Three quick stabs at the buzzer.

'Who is it?' May Lin's voice. Relief flooded through me.

'It's me.'

She opened the door and turned on a light.

'Richard! My God, darling.'

I hadn't allowed for the impact of my appearance. I was white-faced, twitching and clutching a gun and a handful of black lace underwear. 'May Lin,' I gasped, 'are you all right?'

'Yes, of course. I was worried at not hearing from you all day. But I'm fine. What's happened?' A practical female impulse cut through her concern. 'Are those the only clothes you brought? Richard, that's very romantic, but...'

I nearly collapsed into the hallway. She grabbed me and we clung together there for a minute. She smelled and felt wonderful, especially after the unpleasantness of the past few hours. I've been at close quarters with a lot of women in my life, but there was something, well, restorative, about the touch of May Lin's lips. I've never forgotten it. We went down to the car together and hauled back the clothes and records and grog. I realised that I'd eaten nothing since midday, and that my system had been running on coffee, beer, tobacco and adrenalin for almost ten hours.

May Lin did something with the eggs and vegetables and rice that were in the apartment and I wolfed it down along with some of the white wine as I told her about my day. She listened intently and hardly touched the food. When I'd finished eating she broke open a new pack of cigarettes and lit up.

'I spent some of your money on cigarettes,' she said. 'And the rest on vegetables.'

I nodded and lit up the last of my Luckies. 'Tobacco's a vegetable, too,' I said.

After the food and wine we had coffee and some more of our favourite vegetable. May Lin got excited when I told her about Sallust's sister. She wanted to go out there at once. I was feeling mellow and had got around to thinking about the black underwear again.

'I don't know,' I said. 'What if whoever killed Tan is in cahoots with her?'

'At least we could phone.'

'And say what?'

She puffed smoke. 'I don't know. Anything! We can't just sit here, doing nothing.'

'I'll be honest with you, May Lin. I was thinking of doing just that. Tan had got around to the same thought. But it was a bit late for him. If you'd seen him you might think again.'

'No,' she said fiercely. 'I've seen death. I...'

'Where?' I said.

'In San Francisco. I lived there for a few years. There were fights between the Tongs. People got killed, relatives, friends. We Chinese are used to death.'

'So are we Irish,' I said. 'That doesn't mean we go looking for it. *Why* can't you drop it?'

'It will sound foolish,' she said quietly. 'The revolution in this country was so long ago and you, you're an Australian. Was there ever a revolution in Australia?'

I tried to remember the school history books. They were all about English history. A few revolutions there, I seemed to recall, but a long way back and the same people seemed to stay in charge. We had the Eureka stockade, but it was all over in an hour or so. 'I don't think so,' I said.

'I hate the Manchus and the Japanese. I would do anything to keep them from getting control of China.'

'We're fighting the Japs,' I said. 'They'll get beaten.'

'Hah! The Americans will do a deal with the Japanese. They have already done a deal with them.'

'Come on. Pearl Harbor was...'

'Part of a deal to get America into the war. The big corporations will profit and America and Japan and Russia will carve up the world after Germany is beaten.'

I stared at her. All this was well over my head. Looking back, maybe she was right, in a cockeyed way. In any case, she wasn't going to listen to any arguments, even if I'd had any. There's only one way to deal with a fanatic—retreat and negotiate.

'Okay,' I said. 'I understand. China forever. Okay. I'm not going to kid you, love. I'm scared of what we're up against here.'

It was the first time in my life I'd told a woman I was afraid. There was no doubt, I was crazy in love with her. We were sitting on the sofa and had drawn apart as we talked. Now she came close and put her hand on my cheek. 'You said "we".'

I nodded. 'I'm with you. But we have to be careful. I'll call Beatrice Trudeau and play it by ear. That's if she answers.'

'What if she doesn't?'

'We go to bed and make love. Tomorrow I try to find Pete McVey and his great big gun. Deal?'

'Deal,' she said. 'Now dial.'

I dialled the Pasadena number. It rang in the way that tells you no-one is going to answer. I held the handpiece for May Lin to listen.

'Okay,' she said. 'You win. But tomorrow we find her, with or without McVey.'

'Right. But tonight...'

'I told you you'd won. The underwear?'

I nodded. 'You mind?'

She kissed me, hard. 'I'm no blushing virgin, Richard, you know that. I played around with a guy once who told me in the end that what he really wanted was to do it with my shoes. I minded that. There didn't seem to be any point in being in the room. But if you want to lift and lower a little silk and lace, that's fine with me. In fact, I'll love it.'

'Maybe you'd like me to keep my hat on,' I said.

In the morning, I rang Pete McVey's number in Santa Barbara and got nothing. I called Bobby Silk's office and got Miss Dupre, his personal secretary and my personal enemy. She liked me when I was in work. I asked her if Bobby was in and she said no, which didn't necessarily mean anything. I asked if he'd received a communication from Mr Peter McVey lately and she said she thought so.

Paper rustled. 'Is yesterday lately?'

'Yes.'

'He sent a telegram from San Francisco asking for more money. Mr Silkstein told me to ignore it.'

'What's the address?'

'Jack Tarr hotel.'

She gave me the number. I thanked her, hung up and called the Jack Tarr. May Lin was in the shower; I could hear the water running. I thought about a few of the things we'd done in the night. I wondered if lipstick washed off easily. The phone rang a long time, then Pete's voice came through like a buzz saw with a broken tooth.

'Yeah?' He coughed rackingly. 'McVey.'

'Pete? It's Browning. You sound like hell.'

'I drank too much last night. Chinese whisky. You calling for Silkstein?'

'No, he's dropped the Sallust case. He's lost interest. How far did you get?'

'Nowhere. The Cheng broad left for Hawaii yesterday. I was asking for more dough to follow her.'

'He won't give you any. Listen, Pete, it's got very sticky this end. People are dead.'

'Who?'

'Charles Tan, for one.'

'He wasn't people in my book. You still on it?'

'Sort of, yes. I need your help.'

'Who're we working for?'

I glanced up as May Lin came out of the bathroom. She was naked, rubbing at her hair. The lipstick had gone. Her small, tight breasts were lifted up high; her body was the colour of Australian beach sand and her eyes glittered green in the morning light. I almost dropped the phone.

'Browning? You there?'

'Yes, Pete. Yes, I'm here. I'm... ah, getting five hundred a week from Paramount. I guess we could be working for me.'

'I don't follow.'

May Lin came across the room, walking tiptoe on bare feet, and kissed me. She bent and tickled my left ear with the hard bud of her right nipple.

'Don't worry, Pete,' I mumbled. 'Just get back here. I'm at the Bryson...'

'The Bryson! What happened to the Wilcox?'

The nipple moved around towards my mouth. 'I'll explain. The Bryson. Leave now. You'll be here at three, right?'

'Make it two,' Pete said. 'This I gotta see.'

I dropped the phone. I opened my mouth to receive May Lin's thrusting breast. She danced away from me on those high-arched feet. I lurched after her and caught her in the bedroom.

'Underwear?' she said.

I reached for her. 'To hell with underwear.'

The phone rang. May Lin suddenly looked serious; she waved at me. 'Go.'

I went. That woman could make me do anything, up, down and sideways. I grabbed the phone and barked, 'Yes?'

It was Loren Duke, the Texan. 'Browning?' he drawled. 'Hope I'm not interrupting anything.'

I had to go to the studio for a briefing from Joe Herman and Farrow on how our little deception was shaping. We met in an office in the administration building. They were satisfied. I wasn't very interested, except when they mentioned the Australian trip.

'That still on the cards?' I said.

Farrow frowned. 'You sound too American.'

'I can fix that, mate,' I said. 'Over-bloody-night, if I have to. How about it? She still a goer?'

'That's better,' Farrow said.

Herman puffed cigar smoke. 'Yes. It is a good idea. Some details to work out still. Mr Browning, you were seen talking to some writers in the commissary the other day.'

'So?' I said.

Herman's fat face reminded me of Buddha statues I'd seen in Chinese restaurants. 'What were you talking about? Not this project, I hope.'

Herman had hired Sallust to write whatever he liked, on salary. And now here he was, masterminding this charade. Was there a connection? I took a chance. 'No, Mr Herman,' I said. 'We were talking about Chinese history. Recent history, that is.'

Herman raised his cigar and took a draw. He expelled the smoke in a long plume. If it meant anything, I sure as hell didn't know what it was.

21

I was all through at the studio by one-thirty and I told Loren Duke I was going to have a late lunch in the commissary. He ambled off to look at some horses, maybe eat with them. I drove out of the car park fast and headed back to Wiltshire, thinking that May Lin and I might have time for a quick one before Pete McVey arrived. There was a smash-up on Melrose and the traffic was slowed to a crawl. I sweated and smoked and cursed bad drivers. It was close to three when I got to the Bryson and Pete was already there. That is to say, he was parked in his Packard across the street. When he saw the Olds he got out and waved at me. I swung the car into the parking lot and came back out to the street on foot.

We shook hands. McVey had a three-day stubble and was wearing what looked like a five-day shirt. He smelled of neglect and looked hungry and thirsty.

'Browning,' he said, 'you look like you're doing okay. You keeping honest?'

'Trying to. Come on up and I'll introduce you to my razor and some soap.'

The desk man was back on duty. He'd now seen me in the company of a Texan, a Chinese and a hobo. He must've been wondering what next. We went up to the apartment and May Lin opened the door. I half expected McVey to go for his gun, but he took off his hat instead. Maybe he was too tired for gunplay.

'Mr McVey,' May Lin said.

Pete said, 'Ma'am,' and turned to look at me.

I shrugged. 'Life is strange.'

'Ain't it though.' McVey lapsed into his country boy role as he entered the apartment. He looked at the carpet and clean walls and windows as if he'd never seen the like before. 'You said something about a razor and soap.'

I pointed to the bathroom. 'I can probably find you a shirt as well. Might be a bit snug.'

'Your size'd be fine,' Pete said. 'I've lost some weight.'

He had too. I caught a glimpse of his bony back as I tossed a shirt into the bathroom. May Lin made some coffee in the time off she got from kissing me. We sat in the kitchen, smoking and smiling at each other.

'I tried the number again,' she said.

'And?'

'Nothing. Then I got to thinking. You said she was a librarian. So I rang a few libraries. She works at the public library in Los Feliz.'

'Closer than Pasadena,' I said.

'Yes. But she called in sick three days ago. She said she had a cold and needed a day in bed.'

'Colds can be a bitch,' I said.

May Lin stubbed out her Tarelton. 'Right. They usually don't stop you answering the phone, though.'

We filled Pete in on this little development when he came out of the bathroom with his face shaved, his hair wet, and one of my best shirts almost fitting him. I was feeling a bunch of mixed emotions—besotted by May Lin, glad to have McVey at my side, even if he did seem a little frayed at the edges, and apprehensive about what we might encounter in Pasadena. It would have been nicer to be able to play along with the studio fairy tale, take the trip to Australia, come back by some slow, safe means of transportation. Business before pleasure, but Pete had asked the right question. Whose business was it?

He didn't like to ask, but he needed money for gas. I gave him some. We checked our guns, put on our hats and left the apartment. I was glad to see that McVey still had his big piece and plenty of ammunition. May Lin was wearing wide-leg slacks, medium heels and a silk blouse. She had a light, Chinese-style jacket around her shoulders. No gun. Pete said he'd taken the train back to Santa Barbara and collected the Packard there. He must have been very low on funds because the needle was on empty. We gassed up and headed for Pasadena. Pete drove.

'No offence, Ma'am,' he said after a mile or two, 'but I'm not sure you should be along.'

I knew that was a waste of breath. 'Might need a woman's touch,' I said.

In the 1940s, as now, Pasadena seemed to be mainly mansions, but that was an illusion. There were back streets and small subdivisions where ordinary folk lived. Not poor folk, but people who worked for a living and could pay a decent rent. It was not unknown for movie stars and executives to park their boyfriends and girlfriends hereabouts. Shakespeare was a narrow street that curved and climbed and wound up almost in Arcadia. Beatrice Trudeau's house was at the Arcadia end. The foothills were only a short scamper away for a lively coyote. The house was a modest brick bungalow set on a block that featured my kind of garden—mostly fruit trees, not much lawn and some identifiable flowers like roses and that kind of stuff. It had a big porch in the front with a waist-high wall. I couldn't help thinking what a good wall it would be to hide behind and shoot from.

The afternoon shadows were long; it was a little too early for the honest people to be back home, a little late for the lunch-time philanderers to be paying calls. Generally speaking, the driveways were empty. Pete passed the house and checked out the rest of the street. It ended in a dirt road that had some kind of gate across it with a sign warning trespassers not to trespass. All the houses were well back from the road and some had high hedges. If you had to go calling on a woman you didn't know, carrying guns and not knowing quite what you were going to talk about, this was a good place to do it.

We parked across Miss Trudeau's driveway. I had to admire McVey's technique. There was a garage at the end of the drive with the rear end of a Dodge or Buick sticking out of it. No chance of it getting away now. Pete looked like he wanted to tell May Lin to wait in the car but she got out before he could open his mouth. I was last out, but I walked up the driveway ahead of May Lin trying to shield her. I was in love, remember. Up the brick steps to the porch. No-one behind the wall. No sound either, apart from birds and insects and the sound of leaves being stirred by a light wind. I wondered if Pasadena meant peaceful[25], because that's certainly what it was just then.

McVey waved to us to stand clear of the door. He flattened himself against the wall beside it and knocked. No answer. Another knock. Same result. Pete tried the handle; it turned and the door opened an inch. He waited, then lifted his finger to his lips. His mime indicated that I should stand guard here while he snuck around the back. I felt very scared all of a sudden. What if Tan's killer was inside with a blowtorch? But May Lin's eyes were on me. I nodded, gestured for her to keep clear of any possible lines of fire and hefted the .38. After a few minutes I heard movement inside the house. Then McVey's voice came from inside the door.

'It's me,' he said. 'Come on in.'

We went inside. It was dark and had a shut-up smell, as if no windows or doors had been opened for a week.

'Is she here?' May Lin said.

McVey gestured with his gun towards the back of the house. 'Yup.'

We trooped down a passage that had two rooms off it, into a sitting room and then the kitchen. The place was a complete contradiction—a neat, formal arrangement that looked as if a hurricane had hit it. Everything was in a shambles—dresser doors and drawers opened and smashed, glasses and crockery shattered, kitchen linen in shreds, cookbooks likewise. The surprising thing was the number of gin bottles lying around—there must have been a dozen or so, also a few fifths of Wild Turkey and quite a few short dogs of muscatel. All the bottles were empty.

I picked one up and sniffed it. It hadn't been empty long. 'Sallust?'

McVey shook his head. 'Naw. This is a woman's drinking. You ever notice that? When a woman drinks she soaks up everything in sight?'

'For God's sake,' May Lin almost screamed, 'where is she?'

Pete pointed to a door that led to an enclosed section of the back porch. I opened the door. The area had been partly built in with lining board and there were a couple of big sliding windows with insect-proof screens across them. The room caught the sun in the afternoon and it was still hot even though the direct sunlight had gone. There were closely-packed bookshelves, a desk, a cane easy chair and a single bed. It was a room set up for reading and writing. Beatrice Trudeau was lying supine on the bed. I recognised her from the one time I'd met her several years before. She'd changed; she'd grown more angular and harsh-faced. Mind you, she wasn't looking her best. She wore a floral print dress and a knife was sticking through one of the flowers, right above her heart. A stain spread around her like another flower, a big, dark red one.

May Lin gasped and drew back. I stepped aside and let her retreat. I forced myself to examine the dead woman closely. There was bruising on her face and arms and a trickle of blood from her nose had dried on her upper lip among the dark hairs that almost gave her a moustache. There were marks on the skirt of her dress that looked like liquor spills. I touched the stain on the bedspread. It felt damp, or nearly so.

McVey was leaning against the door jamb. He lit a cigarette and puffed smoke into the room. 'Thoughts, Dick?' he said.

I shook my head. 'I can't see much. She was drunk. She fought. She got killed. Recently. That's all.'

I heard May Lin retching and the sound of water running into the kitchen sink. She came back, drying her face on a lace handkerchief that looked to be good only for getting a smut out of an eye. 'Why? Who?'

'Them's the questions, all right.' Pete said. 'Why're we here, Dick? I kind of forgot.'

'To talk to Miss Trudeau and see if Sallust left any writing here. But we've been well and truly beaten to the punch.'

McVey jabbed his cigarette at the devastated kitchen. 'Other rooms're like this. Hard to tell if they found anything or not.'

'They?' May Lin said.

McVey shrugged. 'Him, her, them or it, your call.'

I went back into the kitchen. 'Chandler said he'd hide anything where he hid his booze.'

'He'd know,' McVey said.

I scratched my chin and looked around the room. 'I suppose it depends on a lot of things—who you're hiding from, what sort of a house, what sort of booze.'

May Lin lit a cigarette and kept her gaze away from the door to the porch. 'He said he liked a corn whisky jug when he was really on a toot.'

'I'd put that outside,' McVey said. 'It's not inside drinking liquor.'

Pete and I went out the back door, down some steps into the yard. May Lin stayed in the kitchen, blowing smoke through the window over the sink.

'Stuck on her, aren't you?' McVey said.

'Yes.'

'Sure you can trust her?'

I grinned at him. 'I'm not sure I can trust *you*.'

The yard was more a less a duplicate of the front garden—trees and shrubs and vines, mostly fruit-bearing. There was a timber table and a couple of chairs arranged around where bricks and stones and an iron griddle had been set up so that you could cook over an open fire. This was before the barbecue craze and it made a nice, tasteful touch. The block ended in an impenetrable tangle of brush and vine that might have continued up into the foothills. No hiding places though. We went into the garage and looked at the car. It was a '41 Dodge coupé with a garage service sticker on the side window and books on the back seat. The late Beatrice Trudeau's car. There were no obvious dints and scratches so she couldn't have been drinking long. A drunk's car usually looks like the surface of a skating rink—I speak from experience.

Things were pretty orderly inside the garage, not that there were many things. Low workbench, a few tools on shelves, some empty oil cans, a couple of piles of newspapers. More signs of sobriety—a drunk's garage always overflows with empties. Pete prowled around the space, pushing this, kicking at that. He was brushing up against things and getting oil and dirt on his clothes and he didn't care. The garage floor was a series of large concrete slabs and Pete located the edge of each one and tested it for movement with his weight. I made a search of the car, just for something to do. It was clean and well cared for, meaning that there was nothing of interest inside.

'Hey?' Pete's voice sounded a note of hope.

I slammed the car door. 'What?'

Under a pile of burlap sacks he'd found a broken section of slab. He crouched and levered the concrete up with his fingers. It came easily. There was a hollowed-out space underneath it. A grey metal box, about the size of a Webster's Dictionary[26], fitted neatly into the hole. Pete hooked his index finger through the small handle on the top of the box and pulled it clear. The box wasn't locked. Pete opened it and we saw a sheaf of paper within. The top sheet was covered with typescript, much annotated and emended in handwritten blue ink.

'Bingo,' he said.

He closed the box and we left the garage.

I said, 'Chandler was wrong. You wouldn't hide booze in a place like that.'

Pete grinned. 'No. Ray was right. There was a corn liquor jug in the sacks. Come to think of it, maybe I should get it. I could do with a drink.'

He thrust the box at me and I took it in both hands. It was getting dark now, time to switch on the lights in the house. Pete came back with his finger hooked through the ring on the neck of the jug. I looked up at the house, wondering why May Lin hadn't turned on a light. Maybe the power was off. Great; we could sit around and read Sallust's manuscript and drink his whiskey under candlelight. We went up to the house, climbed the steps and entered the kitchen.

'May Lin,' I said, 'we've found something.'

I turned on the light and blinked. Two figures stood clasped together in the middle of the room. A man and a woman. 'Mr Browning,' the man said, 'put the box on the table. Mr McVey, keep your hands where I can see them.'

We both obeyed. There was no point in arguing. The man was Big Sung and he had a pistol up against May Lin's temple.

22

'I am assuming that both of you gentlemen have guns,' Big Sung said. 'I want to see them on the table next to the box within three seconds. If I do not, May Lin dies.'

My hand shook as I took the .38 from its holster. There was plenty of Sung's body visible and I probably could have shot him, but not before he'd blown out May Lin's brains. I put my pistol on the table. 'Did you kill Tan and Beatrice Trudeau?' I said.

'Yes. Regrettably. But you can see why I would not hesitate to kill again. Mr McVey, if you please.'

'Do it, Pete,' I said.

McVey set the jug down at his feet and repeated my action. His great big gun lay on the table, as useless as a garden gnome. Sung moved gracefully. He released May Lin and swept up my .38. He checked it quickly, before Pete or I had time to do anything other than feel relief that May Lin didn't have a gun to her head. Sung now had a gun in each hand.

'I'm sorry,' he said, 'but I think it is necessary for all three of you to die.'

May Lin gasped. 'Sung, you could not kill me. You've known me all my life.'

Sung nodded. An oddly small movement for such a mountainous man. 'And hated you and all your kind.'

'My uncle?'

'Him, perhaps most of all.'

'I don't understand,' May Lin said.

'Me neither.' Pete McVey bent, picked up the jug and pulled the cork. He hooked his finger and swung the jug up in the approved manner and took a swig. He was taking a desperate chance, but he got away with it. 'Appreciate it if you'd tell us a few things before you kill us, brother. What's the harm?'

Sung's face and eyes were without expression. 'Put the jug down or I will shoot you where you stand.'

Pete finished his swig, but he lowered the jug to the floor. 'I just figured something out,' he said.

I was desperate to keep everyone talking. 'What?'

'I was wondering why whoever ripped this room and the others apart didn't tear up the room where the lady's lying. Then it came to me. And I guess a few other things fall into place too.'

Sung seemed almost interested, but the hands holding the guns didn't move a fraction. Handguns are heavy to hold for any length of time, but for a man like Sung that wouldn't matter. He had all three of us well covered and looked as if he could keep it that way as long as he liked.

'What the hell are you talking about, Pete?' I said.

'Did you notice the books in there?' He jerked his head at the enclosed porch.

I hadn't noticed anything in particular about the books, except that there were a lot. I had an impression of sameness, like you'd get from rows of encyclopedias. I said something to this effect.

Pete nodded. 'They're all about Communism—Marx, Lenin and those other jaspers. Must mean something to our friend here, that he didn't turn them into confetti. I guess he ain't interested in the Sun, Moon and Stars gizmo.'

Sung sneered. 'Only to melt it down into bullets.'

May Lin gasped. 'Sung, a Communist? You?'

Sung's huge head dipped forward a fraction in agreement. 'And why not?' he said. 'I was not born into softness and self-indulgence like yourself, May Lin. I was born a peasant, almost a slave. If I had not been big and strong my blood and bones would be manuring some field in China like those of most of my class for a hundred generations.'

'We are working for a new China,' May Lin said softly. 'The old ways are finished. The people...'

'The people will be ground into the dust as they always have been, unless their true representatives hold power. Only through the Communist Party can the people achieve freedom.'

'As in Russia?' May Lin said, scornfully.

'China is not Russia. Things will be different.'

'You are a fool!'

I admit I sucked in a little air when May Lin said that. Brave, of course, but not wise when you're facing a killer with two guns. *Keep the party going, Dick,* I thought. I said, 'Where's Sallust?'

Sung shook his head. 'He had discovered that I was not quite the mindless thug that I seemed. I had to remove him. I feared that he might have written of what he knew. I still think it.'

Everyone except Sung looked at the metal box on the table.

'Took you a while to get here,' Pete said.

'Oh, I did not find out about this place from Sallust. He told me nothing. He died very bravely.'

A chill entered the air.

'I told my uncle,' May Lin said. 'Sung must have learned of it through him. My uncle trusts Sung. He has done so for many years.'

'Chiang Kai-shek and the Kuomintang are no different from the warlords I served in my youth. They are murderers who will grind the faces of the poor just the same.'

'No,' May Lin said.

'What about Sallust's sister?' I said. 'Why did you kill her?'

There was a definite expression on Sung's face now—sadness. 'I did not wish to kill her. When I told her that her brother was dead, she became hysterical. She attacked me. Then she pleaded with me to kill her. She said she would expose me and others, that she would betray the Communist Party of America to the authorities. She had lost her faith. She had turned to drink. Poor woman. I obliged her.'

'And you talk of murderers,' May Lin said.

Sung didn't answer. I had the feeling that we were running out of time. I racked my brain for something to say and only a name surfaced. 'Joe Herman,' I said. 'Does he have anything to do with this?'

Sung lifted the muzzle of my .38 a fraction. 'A good Communist,' he said. 'For a Russian. And now I must ask you to turn around very slowly.'

I was sure this was it. I glanced at May Lin. Her full lower lip was caught in her teeth and her eyes were huge. She had never looked more beautiful. It was only her presence that stopped me falling on my knees and making some kind of plea to Sung. As it was, I closed my eyes and began to turn slowly. May Lin did the same. My heart was crashing in my chest; blood roared so loudly in my head that I knew I wouldn't hear the shots. My mouth and throat dried; I felt my bowels loosening; I didn't want to die but I couldn't do a thing to prevent it.

Pete McVey dived for his gun. Desperation made him lightning fast. He got his hand on it. Everything seemed to move in slow, loopy motion. I saw McVey's finger uncurl as it reached for the trigger. His face was a snarling mask of hate and fear. Then there was an explosion and the top half of Pete's head disintegrated. Sung had used his own gun, which must have had some kind of soft-head load. Total destruction. I wanted to move but I couldn't. I wanted to scream but my throat had seized up.

Sung didn't watch Pete slump to the floor. He pointed the .38 at May Lin's chest. I closed my eyes again.

Two shots shook the walls.

23

The blood that splattered over May Lin, me and the body of Pete McVey was Big Sung's. The shooter was Loren Duke. He stepped from the enclosed part of the porch and for a moment I thought he was going to blow smoke from the muzzle of his pistol. He didn't. He took two steps into the kitchen and looked at Sung, who was flat on his back in a large, but not spreading, pool of blood.

'Not very good shooting,' Duke said. 'Got him in the neck before I hit the heart.'

I was shaking. I grabbed at May Lin, partly to touch her, partly for support. 'It was good enough,' I said. 'Thanks. Pity you were too late to save Pete.'

Duke nodded and touched Sung's shoulder with the toe of his high-heeled boot. 'Gutsy guy. He saved your asses. It's a mite hard to shoot a man in the back without warning, and I sure as hell wasn't going to ask him to turn round.'

May Lin slumped into a chair. I lit cigarettes for the three of us and we smoked for a while before speaking. You see people walk away nonchalant from shoot-outs in the movies. It's not like that. Everyone who survives is in shock. I picked the jug up, found some unbroken glasses and poured three shots. I felt as if I could've drunk the whole lot. The air in the kitchen was filled with the smell of cordite but tobacco smoke was gaining on it.

Duke accepted a second drink, tossed it off quickly and said, 'Phone is where? I gotta call this in.'

'Just a minute,' I said, 'did you hear all that?'

'Sure did. You thought you'd given me the slip, but I followed you from the studio to here. I saw the big Chink—excuse me, Miss—the Chinaman, come out of a hidey hole and I hopped in the little room there. Holy Christ—excuse me again—I like to shit when you started talking about the books. Thought you might all come in and take a look around.'

'I mean, you heard he was a Communist agent of some kind?'

'Helped me to shoot him,' Duke said. 'I hate those bastards.'

May Lin was sitting at the table, smoking and staring straight in front of her. I went over and put my arm around her shoulders. She moved towards me slightly. I caressed her neck. I looked down at Pete McVey and gave him a silent thank you.

'What about Joe Herman?' I said.

Duke was on his way out of the room. He half-turned and grinned at me. 'Now that's a long story. We've had our eye on him for a time. Him and that Film and Photo League[27]. What d'you think I've been doing, hanging around like I have?'

Duke went away to phone. May Lin and I sat together, not talking. Men arrived, not cops, and took the bodies away. Duke said he'd contact Pete's relatives and arrange for his car to be garaged somewhere. He took all the guns. That left the box.

201

'Better take a look,' Duke said. 'Might have something about the Commies we oughta know.'

I opened the box and took out a stack of paper. There were three hundred sheets full of neat typing. It was a novel entitled *The Sin*. Duke and I looked at it without comprehension. How do you find out if there's anything you need to know in three hundred pages? May Lin picked up the manuscript and started flicking through it. She read here and there, glanced backwards and forwards through the typescript before putting it back in the box.

An FBI man was hovering near the door. Duke waved him away. 'Well Miss, what's it about?'

'Incest,' May Lin said.

Duke detailed the waiting agent to drive us back to the Bryson. He said he'd be by to get a full statement from us. We nodded and went, doing what we were told, all the way.

Back at the apartment, May Lin phoned her uncle and told him about Big Sung. She did that in English, then she spoke in Chinese for a while. I looked at her enquiringly when she'd finished.

'I was telling him that we found out nothing about the Sun the Moon and the Stars.'

'Right,' I said. 'Maybe Sue Cheng's going to pick it up in Hawaii.'

'Maybe.' She sat next to me and we kissed. 'I'm sorry about Mr McVey.'

'Me too. He was a good guy. It shouldn't have happened. What about you, darling? Are you going to go on with this treasure hunt?'

She snuggled closer. 'No, Richard. I'm finished with all that. Maybe some of the things Big Sung said were true. Maybe the revolution in China is not really finished. I'm confused and you can't do that kind of work unless you are very sure.'

'Will you be able to pull out, just like that?'

She told me she could, courtesy of Singapore Sam who was a bigger wheel in the Chinese community than I'd realised. She also told me something about her own background—her Chinese father, Australian mother, eastern college education, failed marriage. It took quite a long time and a few cold drinks and we were in bed together by the time she finished. There was no question of making love, and no question of taking our arms from around each other.

'Now, you tell me about you,' she said into my shoulder.

'Take too long,' I said. 'I'm so much older.'

'How much?'

She was thirty-four. I lied and said, 'Ten years. I'll tell you tomorrow.' That would give me time to get a story straight.

She touched me gently in one of the right places. 'That's not so old.'

I was almost asleep. 'A pity about Herman,' I murmured. 'There goes our trip to Australia.'

But it didn't work out like that at all. May Lin and I stayed in the apartment for a couple of days, getting to know each other, making plans and waiting for someone from the studio to come and throw me out. It didn't happen. Our first visitor was Bobby Silkstein, who was polite to me, courtly to May Lin and didn't say anything at all about me going off salary. In fact, he delivered a salary cheque, with bonuses, minus his commission. He took us out to lunch at the Brown Derby and Spencer Tracy came over to our table to say hello. May Lin was very impressed. So was I. Tracy gave me a big Irish wink that I didn't know how to interpret.

Our next caller was Loren Duke. He sat down and took statements from us, writing rapid shorthand. When we'd finished he put the notepad away, accepted a beer and asked us what we wanted to know.

'Will May Lin be in trouble for her activities?' was my first question.

Duke shook his head. 'The US government supports the Nationalist Chinese. 'Course we don't exactly admire to have people running around the country getting up to shenanigans, but I wouldn't worry, Miss Lin.'

'Have you found Hart Sallust?' May Lin said.

'Nope. And I don't reckon we ever will. That Big Sung was a secretive guy. I guess he stashed him somewhere in California. We might run into some of the boys who worked for him and get some information. But it'd be a long shot.'

'Pete McVey and Beatrice Trudeau,' I said. 'Have they been...?'

Duke sipped beer and nodded. 'Cousin of Miss Trudeau came forward, got herself a lawyer and things are getting sorted out. Mr McVey has family in Idaho. They're looking after it.'

There was a small silence after that. Then I said, 'What about Joe Herman?'

Duke smiled, glad to be past the sad bit and onto happier topics. 'Well, we interviewed Mr Herman and I have to admit, we kinda snowed him a little. Said his pal Mr Sung had talked to us. Said we had Mr Sallust safe, like that. Mr Herman got confused and scared. He talked a streak.'

'And?' I said.

'And he came round to our way of thinking. Long and the short of it is, he's going to be working for us now instead of the commies. We've got him by the nads—excuse me, Miss—and he knows it.'

'I don't follow,' I said. 'You mean everything goes on as before—the film and everything?'

'Yup. No change, and we've got a little something for you, Mr Browning, by way of thanks for your co-operation and services.'

I glanced uneasily at May Lin. Was this it? The sting in the tail. I hadn't known the FBI to be magnanimous in my dealings with it so far. Duke opened his briefcase, took out some official-looking papers and handed them across. They were application forms for US citizenship, made out in the name of Richard Kelly Browning and endorsed by Loren P. Duke and someone else whose stamp proclaimed him to be a judge of the district court in the County of Los Angeles in the state of California. I hastily covered up the date of my birth, which they'd got right, and shook Loren Duke's hand. He passed over his gold pen and I signed in the appropriate places.

'This is wonderful,' I said.

'Least we could do. And there's more.' He took a slip of paper from his pocket and read, 'I'm able to tell you that a decree of divorce was granted to Elizabeth Browning, nee MacKnight, under the Matrimonial Causes Act, Commonwealth of Australia, on May 8, 1939.'

I'd told May Lin about my Australian marriage and that I didn't know whether it was still in force. I hadn't told her about the next one, but since that was in 1929, it was invalid so it didn't matter[28]. I reached over and took her hand and didn't say a word. Loren Duke raised his beer in a toast and we drank. He said he'd file the citizenship papers and I could expect a ceremony 'pretty damn soon'. He didn't apologise for saying damn and I let it pass. May Lin and I went to bed and made love for about the fiftieth time, although it felt like the first.

I did some more nonsense at the studio over the next few weeks. Then May Lin and I got married. The Reverend Peter Moon performed the ceremony in a little church off Venice Boulevard. Mrs Tan was there along with Singapore Sam and some more of May Lin's relatives and friends. Loren Duke was my best man and there was a scattering of movie people and journalists and gamblers and drinkers I'd got to know over the years. After a party at

Sam's place we drove to Palm Springs for the honeymoon.

The Desert Sands hotel was a series of well-appointed cabins set around a large swimming pool and surrounded by lush, tropical gardens. It must have taken a million gallons of water a day to get it like that. God knows where they got it from. May Lin and I made love morning, noon and night, took drives out into the desert, ate in the Palm Springs restaurants, played a little golf and swam in the pool. After a week in the sun I was as dark as a Latin. May Lin's smooth ivory skin took on a light tan and that was all. We walked, talked and spent every second together. She admired me and I admired her and we admired ourselves.

One morning I went down to the pool and swam a few laps before lying in the sun with the morning paper. A guy came down in a bathrobe, peeled it off to reveal a stocky, slightly flabby body which looked a lot better when he began doing fancy dives into the pool from the low board. It was Raymond Chandler. When he stopped diving I went up and we got to talking. He'd heard about Pete but didn't know the details. He said he'd miss him and had been sorry to hear what had happened.

'You were more or less right about Hart Sallust's hiding place,' I said. 'He had his jug under some burlap sacks in the garage. He hid other things there, too.'

Chandler puffed on his pipe and nodded. 'I should write something about that one of these days[29].'

'Raymio,' a chirpy voice said, 'who's your young friend?'

Cissie Chandler was wearing a flowing white frock with a wide-brimmed hat and carrying a parasol. She sat down next to Chandler under the sun umbrella and put a camera on the slatted table.

Chandler locked his right index finger around hers, which was cased in a white lace glove. 'This is Mr Browning, darling. I think he came to the house once.'

Cissie peered at me through her tinted spectacles. 'Oh yes,' she said. 'I sent him off to look for you at that awful party from which you returned very drunk.'

Chandler coughed. 'Drying out down here, Browning. Before getting back to work. What brings you here?'

'Just a holiday,' I said. There was something so awful-seeming about the Chandler marriage that I didn't want to refer to mine.

'Uh huh. Where's Taki, darling?'

Cissie ordered an iced tea from the waiter who drifted up. Chandler did the same and I ordered coffee, although I felt like a double scotch.

'Here he is,' Cissie said.

A large, black Persian cat sprang onto the table. It scowled at the waiter when he distributed the cups and glasses. Cissie Chandler took a sip of her iced tea and reached for her camera.

'Let me get one of you and Mr Browning and Taki,' she said. 'You make such a lovely trio.'

I wanted to get out of there as fast as I could, so I reached for the cat. The brute scratched me. I heard

Chandler chuckle just as Cissie snapped the picture. I said the scratch was nothing, drank my coffee and said goodbye. I gave them my address at the Bryson and promised to visit them in LA. I felt a bit guilty about not honouring the promise when I got a copy of the snapshot in the mail a few weeks later, but I still did nothing about it. I heard they moved to La Jolla.

Back in Hollywood, May Lin got work as a script editor and I continued to meet with Herman and John Farrow and play charades. The war started to go better for our side. My citizenship came through and May Lin and I started to talk about buying a house. Towards the end of the year I got a call from Farrow at the Bryson.

'Browning, this is Farrow.'

'Yes, mate?'

He sighed. 'You don't have to lay it on for me. Good news, or bad, depending on how you look at it.'

'Yeah?' I said.

He laughed. 'Yes. Get packed, cobber. You're going to Australia.'

24

Now that we had really got to it, I wasn't so sure. I'd be going to Australia, where there were at least a couple of major criminal charges pending against me, not to mention civil matters, on the say-so of the FBI. Experience had taught me what that was worth. I went home in a state of considerable agitation. May Lin was still at work and I managed to get drunker than I'd intended. When she arrived, she was less than pleased to find me reeling around the apartment babbling about my past misfortunes and present problems.

I don't remember much about the fight we had. I guess I must have spilled too many beans—told her my age, something of my war history, maybe. Unheroic stuff anyway. I don't know what I could have been uncomplimentary about, because I loved her to distraction. Everything she did was fine by me, although I might have said something about her habit of leaving cigarette butts in the bathroom, the smell of the incense she was always burning and the cousins in white suits who kept turning up and borrowing money. The upshot was she walked out, calling me an old, drunken fool. I proceeded to prove her right that night and for the next few following.

She moved back into her Venice apartment. One of the bigger white-suited cousins came and collected her things. I didn't argue. What was the point? I was sick at heart about losing her and scared to death about flying in a military aircraft to Australia. Which pain was the greatest was hard to say. I drank a lot and gambled and quarrelled with people. I was a mess. Bobby Silk offered to fix me up with a girl.

'A redhead,' he said. 'Jugs like this and legs on her like you wouldn't believe.'

'You screw her then,' I said. 'Or is she one of your cast-offs?'

Bobby shrugged. His narrow shoulders were starting to get padded with fat. I wondered if he'd end up a blimp like his old man. 'Suit yourself, Dick. What can I do for you?'

I was due to fly out in two days. We were in his office. The décor was Chinese that season. It didn't help my mood. 'Is there any way I can get out of this piece of bullshit?'

Bobby examined his manicure. 'Don't even think about it. Hey, Dick, you're looking older. That's great for the part.'

'Have I got any money coming?'

'You mean now?'

'Yes.'

Bobby let go a high-pitched laugh which he quickly cut off in favour of a deeper chuckle. 'What you've got is debts, unearned advances, obligations. Polish up your saluting, Dick. That's my advice to you.'

He demonstrated what he meant by snapping off a smart one from where he sat behind his big desk. I nearly hit him.

The B-52 took off from Burbank at 0530 hours, which is early in anybody's language and damn early in mine.

Needless to say, there were no movie people on board. Farrow and Herman had said their goodbyes the day before and there was no sign of Spencer Tracy or Bette Davis. I was decked out in the uniform of a US army captain. Don't ask me why. My travelling companions were a Colonel Westmacott from Alabama, a Major Smith from Washington and a few lower ranks who seemed to be along to keep the brass happy and comfortable. There was the air crew, of course, smooth, confident types as I recall. I was introduced to them but I can't remember their names. The navigator looked like Errol Flynn. That might account for the lapse of memory.

I hadn't done much passenger flying and my own days at the stick were a long way behind me, but nothing seemed to have changed. The plane was noisy, smelly, uncomfortable and cold. We sat strapped into metal and webbing seats, and for amenities we had army blankets, thermos coffee and sandwiches.

'What's our route?' I shouted to Major Smith over the din of the engine and the rattling rivets.

'Hawaii, then Bris-bane.' He produced a map and drew two lines on it with a ballpoint pen. I think this was the first time I'd seen one of these and I guess Major Smith seized every opportunity to demonstrate his. You needed clout to get hold of one. I was too worried to be impressed. I looked at the speck in the middle of the vast ocean, joined by a thin line to the solid mass of Australia. It looked like a hell of a long way. I started to listen to the notes of the engines, worrying when I fancied I could hear a missed beat. But my ears were popping so much and my teeth were chattering so hard I couldn't be sure of anything.

'Understand you're a movie star,' Colonel Westmacott said. 'Brave man to be coming out to the Pacific. Should be more like you 'n' Gable. Have a drink.'

He uncorked a fifth of Early Times bourbon and the trip took an upswing right then. The colonel, the major and the captain flew in to Hawaii the best of friends, toasting Patton and Ike, cursing Hitler and Tojo, and agreeing that we might have to stop the Russkies at the Rhine. In Hawaii I got my first real experience of the American military in operation, as far as the serving officer is concerned. In my time I'd soldiered in Australian, British, Mexican and Canadian armies and I have to say that the Americans put them all to shame—for laying on the good things of life, that is. What the Yanks were like in the field I never found out, thank God.

I was given hot food, beer, coffee and brandy and a cot in a fan-cooled room while they got the plane ready for the next leg. After a quick shower I was feeling in fine fettle as we took off for the hop to Queensland. I was a little surprised to find that Colonel Westmacott wasn't joining us for the flight to Australia. He'd been very enthusiastic about harrying the Japs out of the Pacific.

'Colonel's a desk man essentially,' the major said. 'Me, I'm hoping to see action.'

I nodded. 'Me, too, in a manner of speaking.' I was thinking about the lines on his map. *Well south of the Solomons, and the Japs were beaten there anyway, weren't they? This is a milk run.*

We struck some turbulence six hours out.

The navigator stuck his head out through the cockpit door. 'Hey, guys,' he drawled, 'little dirty weather around here. Buckle up tight and hang on to your drinks.'

I tried to look through the small window behind me but it was running with moisture. We seemed to be in the middle of an endless cloud. It muffled the sound of the engine and I had the feeling that I was floating through space, cut adrift from everything and everybody. Lightning flashed around us and thunder claps shook the plane. It was weird: every man in the personnel section, wedged in between the flight control cabin and the cargo hold, lit a cigarette, simultaneously.

As the tobacco fug mounted the plane began to shake and buck. I wanted to rush into the cockpit and tell these greenhorns what to do, but fear kept me plastered to my seat. Bottles magically appeared, quite a few of them. We passed them backwards and forwards and the cigarettes and differences in rank seemed to disappear. We were all bent on demonstrating our lack of fear. My guts were churning and my hands shook. One of the Yanks started singing 'Begin the Beguine' and I joined in. Then I realised that my voice had developed a squeak and I shut up.

After a while everyone fell silent. The plane dropped, sickeningly, through hundred-foot air pockets and was buffeted by screaming winds. The noise of the storm drowned out the engines. From time to time the windows were filled with blue and yellow lightning from flashes that seemed to miss us by inches. Then there was a crash and the plane seemed to twist on its axis and drop a thousand feet in a second. The lights in the cabin went out.

Someone said, 'Lightning strike,' and the next sound I heard was two fear-choked voices praying.

The nose had dropped and we were heading down, but not spinning. Some instinct told me not to stay there buckled into a metal seat with the resistance of a soup can. I undid my belt and felt my way back towards the cargo hold. The payload was bolted to stanchions riveted to the floor and strapped down with metal hawsers. I found a space between two large, anchored and lashed-down crates. I crawled in there and crouched with my head on my knees.

The storm howled and the engines screamed. Lightning crackled; my hidey-hole was lit up for brief, flaring seconds. I could read the stencilling on the crates—US NAVY, BELT FEED, .45, × 50 000. Crouched there in the dark, I wondered what the hell it meant. It came to me at the moment the plane shuddered from end to end as if a rocket had hit it. Ammunition! I was wedged in between thousands of rounds of live ammunition. It was almost funny. I almost laughed. Then all sound ceased; there was a gliding sensation that was more frightening than the deafening noise. I curled up like a foetus. I might have prayed, I don't remember. I heard a noise like the crack of a thousand stockwhips and everything went dead silent, still and black.

I sometimes think that death is the only significant experience I've not had—ecstasy, misery, wealth, impoverishment, imprisonment, torture, critical illness, brilliant success—I've had 'em all, except the big one. I *thought* I'd had it then, when the B-52 came down and, as I slowly came back to my senses, my first reaction was almost of irritation. *Jesus Christ,* I thought muddle-headedly, *will I have to go through all this again?* This was replaced quickly by relief. Then terror. The plane was down and I was still cuddled up to several tons of explosive substance. I wriggled out of the space without even wondering whether any part of me was broken. Nothing was. I had a stiff neck, a sore shoulder and a pounding headache, but I was intact. I was drenched in sweat but I couldn't feel any flowing blood.

I crawled out. The front section of the plane was a mausoleum. The cockpit had been driven back into the personnel section, which had been penetrated by several tree branches. The metal seats had come adrift and the ribs of the aircraft had collapsed inwards, slicing and spearing men. I saw three bodies and parts of several more. I was whimpering with fear as I crawled past them towards a faint light—a gaping hole in the side above the port wing, or where the wing should have been. It had been sheared off on impact. I heaved myself up to the hole and gazed through it at dense jungle, shrouded in grey mist. The edges of the hole were razor sharp and I'm pretty sure I was weeping as I draped a couple of blankets and major Smith's greatcoat over the metal. I knew the major wouldn't be needing it— his head was no longer attached to his body.

Somehow I managed to climb out, steady myself on the stub of the wing and work my way back to where

I could jump to the ground. If I was game. It was almost dark and I'd be jumping an uncertain distance onto an uncertain surface. Then I thought about the ammo and I jumped. I came down on a huge springy fern, fought free of its damp, sticky fronds and got my feet onto solid ground. In the last of the daylight I could see that the plane had clipped a big outcrop of rocks, slewed around and ploughed its way down through a thick stand of towering trees. It had come to rest with its nose flat against more rocks. The body of the plane, minus one wing and penetrated in various places by tree trunks and branches, lay on a high rock shelf . From my flying days I knew that the only sensible thing to do with downed aircraft was to get clear of them. Fuel leaks, sparks, electrical connections, hot metal ignition—anything could happen at any time.

I battled my way through the undergrowth, scratching my hands and face, falling, stumbling and looking back over my shoulder. Rain began to fall, which lessened the chance of an explosion. I was a hundred yards away and sheltered behind a thick tree before I considered myself safe. I had a desperate wish for a drink and a crying need for a smoke.

'To celebrate,' I said out aloud and giggled.

Then the sound died in my throat. A party of men emerged from the jungle, small, neat shapes, moving purposefully towards me. I pressed back against the tree but there was no chance of escape—they'd seen and heard me. I strained my eyes in the gloom. They were so small, almost the size of schoolboys. But they were carrying carbines and wore uniforms—soft caps with peaks, leggings. The one in front held up his hand and the rest stopped. He spoke.

At first I thought the language was Chinese, having heard a fair bit of it recently. Then I realised my mistake. Japanese!

I threw up my hands. 'American,' I babbled. 'No, Australian. Oh, God. Friend! Friend!'

NOTES

As foreshadowed in the introduction to the last volume of Richard Browning's memoirs, published as *Browning in Buckskin,* problems have arisen with the old actor's taping technique and mental condition. Browning appears to have entered a period of alcoholic disturbance after his recollection of choosing, in 1938, *Sante Fe Trail* over *Gone With the Wind* as a vehicle for his acting talents.

Subsequent experiences were equally unfortunate. The series of cassettes which document his activities over the next two years are chaotic and all but indecipherable. Like other resident aliens in the USA, Browning experienced difficulties with the immigration authorities. Readers of *Browning in Buckskin* will recall that he struck a deal with FBI agent Groom over this matter which appeared to guarantee him security of residence. The FBI however, as will not surprise any student of the Bureau's history, reneged on the deal and Browning was once again under threat.

On Tape 20/ii Browning's voice and purpose become clear again. The subject he embarked upon interested him and he struggled to recollect the experience and communicate it accurately.

Browning appears to have remained sober for a matter of weeks and these tapes are the most coherent and organised so far encountered in the collection. Very little editorial intervention has been needed. Despite his disclaimers, there are indications that Browning had familiarised himself with the prose style of the American hard-boiled writers. Perhaps he read stories in magazines like *Black Mask* or *Dime Detective.* On some of the tapes a sound can be heard which appears to be the turning over of pages. Perhaps he studied scripts or listened attentively to the voice-over in the many private eye movies he claimed to have watched. Whatever the source, there are indications in this portion of Browning's long memoir, as in no other so far transcribed, of outside literary influences.

Of interest is a faded and creased photograph, annotated on the back, 'RC & Taki, Palm Springs 1943', found among Browning's ill-kept collection. It shows him in the company of a stocky, bespectacled man who is unmistakably Raymond Chandler. The cat which Browning has evidently been holding has scratched his face and his hands are up, covering the wound. Chandler gazes fondly at the cat.

A number of references have been consulted to check on the authenticity of Browning's account. In particular, Frank MacShane's *The Life of Raymond Chandler* (Cape, 1976) and his edition of the *Selected Letters of Raymond Chandler* (Columbia University Press, 1981) have proved essential. Also of great value were *Raymond Chandler Speaking,* edited by Dorothy Gardiner and K. S. Walker (Four Square ed., 1966) and *The Inquisition in Hollywood,* by Larry Ceplair and Steven England (University of California Press, 1983).

1. Flynn is misquoting from the celebrated poem 'My Country' by Dorothea McKellar. More accurately:
   I love a sunburnt country
   A land of sweeping plains

2. Browning was misinformed. Canada did not send *draftees* overseas until later in the war, but regular soldiers and volunteers were serving abroad at this time.

3. A pavlova is a dessert made from a circular meringue filled with whipped cream and topped with fruit, usually passionfruit.

4. Preston Sturgess (1898–1955) was a screenwriter and director, best known for light comedies such as *The Great McGinty*, *The Lady Eve*, *The Palm Beach Story*, etc.

5. The Garden of Allah was a hotel on the southwest corner of Sunset and Crescent Heights Boulevards. Silent screen actress Nazimova built a house on the site and later the bungalows that comprised the hotel's accommodation. There were many famous guests over the years and the bar was at one time known as the 'Algonquin Round Table West' in recognition of the writers and wits such as Dorothy Parker, Scott Fitzgerald and Robert Benchley who drank there.

6. *Lost Weekend* was indeed an Academy Award winner. The film won four Oscars for best picture, actor, director and screenplay. Browning's name does not appear in the credits.

7. 'Sugar Ray' Robinson was welterweight and middleweight boxing champion of the world at various times through the 1940s and 50s. He fought many hundreds of bouts in a long career, losing few. Many experts consider him, pound for pound, the greatest fighter in the history of boxing.

8. Browning probably refers to Warner Oland (1880–1938), a Swedish actor who specialised in playing Orientals. He played Chinese detective Charlie Chan in sixteen films.

9. See *'Box Office' Browning*, pp. 79–81.

10. Browning is referring to experiences at public school. He appears to be identifying himself as the kind of bully who extorted money from smaller boys. Raymond Chandler attended Dulwich College in London, a public school perhaps on a par with Browning's alma mater—Dudleigh Grammar.

11. The Sydney Harbour Bridge is a single-span bridge linking the south to the north shores. It was opened in 1932 and crosses approximately five hundred metres of water. The tray of the bridge is fifty-three metres above sea level and daredevil flyers have flown small aircraft through this space.

12. See *'Beverly Hills' Browning*, pp. 38–9. *The Leather Pushers* was an undistinguished boxing film which starred Richard Arlen. Released in 1940, it was shot in 1939, before Browning went to Canada.

13. Australian slang for a person of puritanical outlook.

14. To date, this is the only reference to Browning's brother Thomas, b. 1889, in the memoirs. It is to be regretted that Thomas Browning's trade or profession are not identified, but perhaps later tapes will provide the answer. The implication is of some high-minded calling.

15. See *'Beverly Hills' Browning*, Chapter 16 ff.

16. A lamington is a sponge cake with chocolate or strawberry icing covered with desiccated coconut. The cake is cut up into cubes of approximately two inches square.

17. This reference raises the possibility that Chandler was using McVey as a source for his aborted novel, later a screenplay, entitled *The Blue Dahlia*. In this story a veteran has a plate in his head and experiences headaches much as McVey describes.

18. Victor McLaglen (1886–1959) was an Englishman who spent some of his youth in Australia where he worked as a gold miner and tent boxer. He appeared in many Hollywood films acting in an expressionistic style that was outdated by the 1940s.

19. A bowyang is a piece of string tied around the bottom of the trouser legs worn by bush workers and tramps to stop the trousers from flapping. The bunyip is a mythical beast from Aboriginal legends.

20. See *Browning in Buckskin*, pp. 162–92

21. Browning is right. Although the Gallipoli campaign has become an icon of Australian military history, its actual aftermath saw a decline in the numbers of young men offering themselves for military service. The response of the Australian government was, first, to send a personal letter headed 'A Call to Arms' from W. M. Hughes, the Prime Minister, to every man of military age, second, to bring on a referendum seeking support for conscription. See, Frank Crowley (ed.) *A Documentary History of Modern Australia*, Vol. 4 (Nelson, 1978), pp. 248–52, 266–74. See also *'Box Office' Browning*, pp. 44–64.

22. The books of Arthur Upfield (1888–1964), an Englishman who lived most of his life in Australia, were particularly popular in the US in the 1930s and 40s. Upfield wrote about the outback. His novels featuring the part-Aboriginal detective Napoleon Bonaparte were serialised in the *Saturday Evening Post* and enjoyed a wide readership.

23. The gangster, 'Machine Gun' Jack McGurn adopted an Irish name for his boxing career. His real name was James Vincenzo De Mora. Browning encountered him in Chicago during the prohibition era. See *Browning Takes Off*, p. 222. Australian lightweight and welterweight champion Victor Patrick Lucca fought as Vic Patrick. He was a highly ranked contender for the world lightweight championship but never fought for the title. He was beaten only four times in fifty-five contests. Beau

Jack was generally recognised as world lightweight champion, although the matter was in some dispute at the time Browning is recalling.

24. See *Browning in Buckskin*, p. 181

25. In fact, the word is a corruption of 'pasadero', meaning corridor or gateway, probably in recognition of the town's position at the foot of the San Gabriel mountains.

26. Perhaps another sign of Browning preparing himself to record this part of his memoirs.

27. The Film and Photo League was a small, Communist-backed, film production organisation in the 1940s which produced some films with left-wing content and bias. See, Larry Ceplair and Steven Englund, *The Inquisition in Hollywood* (University of California Press, 1983), pp. 53, 73, 318–19.

28. See, *Browning in Buckskin*, pp. 16–17.

29. In Chandler's 1944 story, 'A Couple of Writers', an alcoholic writer hides his whiskey jug under burlap sacks in the garage. See *Raymond Chandler Speaking*, ed. by Dorothy Gardiner and K. S. Walker (Four Square edition, 1966), pp. 89–105.